BELOVED OF MY 27 SENSES

Beloved *of* My Twenty - seven *Senses*

KAREN FASTRUP

TRANSLATED FROM THE DANISH BY

TARA F. CHACE

BookThug   Toronto   *MMVIII*

first English edition

The translation of the book was made possible by the generous support of
the Danish Arts Council Translation Pool.

Author photo by Morten Holtem
Translator photo by Libby Lewis

Printed in Canada

Library and Archives Canada Cataloguing in Publication

Fastrup, Karen, 1967-   Beloved of my 27 senses / Karen Fastrup ;
translated from the Danish by Tara F. Chace.

Translation of Mine 27 sansers elskede. ISBN 978-1-897388-20-4

   I. Chase, Tara F.
   II. Title.
   III. Title: Beloved of my twenty-seven senses.

PT8177.16.A88M5513 2008   839.81'38   C2008-900632-1

For Malte and Selma

I shuddered to see a face from the inside,
but far, far more I feared
the bare, wounded head without a face.

– Rainer Maria Rilke
The Notebooks of Malte Laurids Brigge

ॐ The crust of the desert in the salt depression was milky white. But even here by the cistern and the little mud brick house with the annex behind it, it was white. The crust. It was salt. Salt that settled on the sand like skin.

Harun tended the cistern, and he did it enthusiastically. Every day he crawled down into it with a bucket fastened to his belt. He knew the stones and exactly where to put his feet. The further down he went, the less oxygen there was in the air. And the surface of the water was often low, not far from the centre of the earth it seemed to Harun.

He placed the palm of one hand on the surface of the water and it rippled beneath his hand. That was how they greeted each other, Harun and the water. Then he skimmed the surface for dust, insects and other small animals.

Then he crawled up again, drew the air down deep into his lungs and emptied the bucket.

The salt caravans passed by here. Weary men watered their animals and drank. The caravan from Ma'tan as-Sarra in Libya came during the day and usually moved on right away, but the one from Chad came at night. The men watered their camels, hobbled their forelegs so they wouldn't run away, lit a bonfire, and slept for a few hours before moving on the next morning.

But on this day there weren't any camels waiting by Harun's cistern. There were two Jeeps. And in the annex a man was lying on rugs that had been spread out over the dirt floor. The skin on his face was wet, and his body trembled at regular intervals.

It was Leo. Anna was sitting with his head in her lap and her doctor's bag by her side. Peter was standing over her, leaning against the wall with his

1

arms crossed. And, outside, in the narrow strip of shade under the eaves, sat Clemens, leaning his back and head against the house.

Then he hid his face in his hands. His head felt like a pitcher of water freezing, and he could feel the veins icing up. Clemens was terrified that soon the ice would burst through his skin, his face would crack, and the meaty fibres behind it would show.

Clemens jumped up.

"Anna!" he yelled.

That night the caravan from Chad came, and the next morning Clemens moved on with it.

 Clemens and Anna were driving out into the desert from Asyût in the British Jeep they'd picked up in Cairo. The car was packed full of boxes and suitcases of cooking utensils and canned goods, books and note pads, carpets and tools; and under the brown canvas on the roof were tents and cots and sleeping bags and large containers of water and gasoline.

There was a fairly good road from Asyût to El-Khârga and on to Mût. A distance of about five hundred kilometres. After Mût there were only caravan routes. One to the northwest and one to the southwest. The southwest route ran through the Libyan Desert by the Gilf el-Kebîr and crossed the border into Libya at 'Ain Doua.

This was the route they would take.

Clemens was a geologist, and he had been selected by the Danish Geological Society to lead this expedition, whose purpose was to map and date the desert sediments northeast of the Gilf el-Kebîr. The other expedition members were Peter, who had done extensive work with fossils and flint concretions in the Sierra Nevada, and Leo, whom Clemens had met for the first time in 1956 in Dakhla and Farâfrah when he had gone on the Qattâra Depression expedition. Most of all, Clemens remembered the sound of Leo: laughing and whistling. Sinatra.

Anna was a doctor, but formally her status on the expedition was as a volunteer because the Danish Geological Society did not set aside funds for expeditions to bring along their own doctors.

In Asyût, Clemens and Anna had purchased the things they didn't think they'd be able to get out in the desert towns.

3

It was quite late when they reached Asyût and the only room they could find for the night was in a wretched hotel across from the train station. The Mehit-Nedemet, the north wind, howled through the streets, causing the few lanterns there to swing back and forth so they cast a flickering light on the dilapidated walls of the buildings. All night long big diesel locomotives were shunting people back and forth. Lots of people were shouting and grumbling over there, in the cold light of the station.

When it was finally morning, Anna and Clemens left the hotel and walked down to the bazaar. After drinking tea with sweet goat's milk and eating sliced oranges and kneaded date paste, they succeeded in finding a couple of hurricane lamps, some water filters, a tiny bit of chlorine powder, a couple of extra pots, some palm rope, and a big block of soap. After each transaction they had to wait for the boy, sent to the nearest bar by the proprietor, to return holding a brass tray with three glasses and a blue pot of scalding hot tea.

After that they left the Valley of the Nile behind them and set out into the desert.

The road stretched in a perfect line through the yellow sand. For the first few kilometres out of the valley it was paved, but the asphalt was crackled like the glaze on an old porcelain vase, and the desert sand was pushing its way up through the cracks so they were driving on a mosaic of black and gold.

It was hot, and Anna and Clemens had rolled down the windows on both sides of the Jeep. The sand settled like a golden film over the black instrument panel. Anna ran a finger through it, and a desert road of sorts cut through the yellow sand parallel to the windshield.

"Why don't we close the windows," she suggested.

"Then we'll roast."

"But what about the sand?"

"You have to get used to the sand," Clemens said. "The wind brings it to life."

Anna tried to brush the sand off the moist palms of her hands, but the tiny grains just dug deeper into her skin.

Clemens smiled.

"Give it up!" he said.

Anna peered at the palms of her hands and then buried her hands between her thighs.

"The sand gets in everywhere," Clemens continued, wiping the worst of it off the windshield with an old cotton rag. "The grains are tiny, only 0.05 to 2 millimetres in diameter."

Anna ran her index finger down over the inside of the door and contemplated the glittering dust.

"What is it actually?" she asked.

"Sand," he said matter-of-factly.

"Yeah, but I mean –"

"Mostly it's quartz. But there's also feldspar and magnetite and garnet." He groped for his sunglasses on the dash. "And calcite and white mica and glauconite," he continued.

Anna wasn't listening anymore. She was staring out at the heat waves shimmering over the desert. "It's like we're driving across an enormous body," she said quietly. "A dead body."

Clemens rested his hand on her thigh. She took it and guided it up to her face.

"In El-Khârga we'll meet Leo and Peter," he said. "And we'll find a cook too."

She nodded.

"Then there'll be five of us," he said. "It won't be so lonely out here then."

"Even if there were five hundred of us, I would still feel lonely out here," Anna said.

Clemens wiped the sand off the windshield, and then put his hand back on the wheel.

After a bit he yelled, "Damn it!"

A ridge of sand had swept across the road in front of them. It originated in the lee of a cluster of low rocks and extended from there outward and upward into a sharp crest that dropped away precipitously. In places the crest of the ridge undulated a little, and the furrows in its surface were convoluted like the ridges in a fingerprint.

Clemens shut off the engine and hopped out. He stood in front of the ridge of sand, sizing it up. Then he went around to the tailgate of the Jeep and took out the two shovels that were strapped there; he tossed one to Anna.

"Here," he said, walking up to the sand.

He started digging with arduous but rapid motions. Anna looked at him for a minute, but then got down to work next to him.

"It could've been much higher," Clemens said.

Anna nodded.

After an hour, Clemens climbed back in behind the wheel, started the engine and drove toward the gorge they'd dug in the sand dune. The Jeep slowed before the wheels started spinning and finally came to a stop. Clemens jumped out and called to Anna who was standing behind the car.

"You drive!" he yelled. "And I'll try to push."

Anna climbed in and put the car in gear while Clemens focused all his weight against the tailgate.

"Go forward a little!" he yelled. "And then backward!"

Anna put the car alternately in first gear and reverse until the wheels made reasonably firm tracks barely a metre long.

"And now first gear, Anna!" he yelled. "And then go for it. But it needs to have traction!"

Anna was sweating and working her way forward and back with the gears. And after a while the tires held and she got free and Clemens ran over and sat down in the passenger's seat. He smiled at her. Then he grabbed the rag from the dashboard and dried his sopping wet face, which was now streaked with sand and dust.

EL-KHÂRGA, NOVEMBER 1996

&> Now I know where my father is. And my mother.

I've been sitting here at the Trans-Saharan Hotel in El-Khârga for over a month, and I get daily updates on the investigation from the embassy in Cairo, which I've been calling every morning, and from Hamad down at the Provincial Office.

The embassy is pouring money into this, also the Danish Foreign Ministry, as soon as I made it clear to them that my parents' disappearance was connected to a scientific expedition, like the many others the ministry noted they'd been on before, and – well, yes – in my father's case that he'd led. Or rather, I made it clear to them that they disappeared in connection with their scientific work. To stick as close to the truth as possible.

And now, as I said, the search party has been gone for a month, led by Hamid Said Ahmad who's a retired major in the Egyptian army and mostly makes his living now by guiding tourists out into the desert, seven days on camelback or in a four-wheel drive vehicle. And if anyone knows the desert out here, they say he's your guy.

But now I know they're looking in the wrong place, they're looking north and northwest of Abu Ballâs, but my mother and father are farther away, they're near Bîr el Shaq. Ugh, this is insane, totally insane! These are old people we're talking about, my mother and father, Clemens is seventy-one and Anna is sixty-seven.

But they're tough, especially my dad, I mean, whatever you do, don't think we're talking about some feeble old man, he's lean and strong and he has a crazy amount of stamina. Much more than my mother – not that she's not strong, quite the opposite, and she certainly has her share of stamina, but she's

7

erratic. Like the khamsin wind. My father used to call her Khamsin when I was a kid, the khamsin is always lurking out there somewhere or other, and then suddenly it will pick up and ravage everything, pummeling the world with dust and sand, raising the temperature by twenty degrees in just a few hours. In the winter it can trigger cloudbursts and make the water course through the cracked wadis like a deluge. That's what she's like, my mother. A khamsin.

And now she's gone after my father. I don't know if she's found him out there. But she knew where to look. And she was the only one, until I realized this morning that I also knew.

I'm always wandering down to see Hamad and ask if there's any news, and especially making phone calls and more phone calls, also Mette, my wife, who thinks the whole thing is completely crazy, two old people heading out into the desert, completely alone, one after the other. And what can I do other than admit that she's right and ask her to water the plants in their house in Lyngby and rummage around out there in their papers and notes and diaries. And then send everything she finds down here to me.

That's how I figured out where they are, by reading page after page of scientific notes, diary entries, all sorts of things they jotted down, and then my mother's... Well, hmm, what would you even call that kind of thing?

And then of course they've also told me things, obviously, as parents are wont to do with their children, about their lives, and there's other things I've managed to guess – my dad would probably say I've deduced – through careful observation of processes and occurrences in their lives and things they've written. I've been able to perceive certain patterns, and, based on those, been able to detect other patterns, or at least get a sense for how these patterns would change over time, sort of feel my way along, just like melt water running down a mountainside in the springtime. One can predict with reasonable accuracy what the water's course is going to be, around the big rocks and high ground, following the gradient down into the ravines and gorges. But sometimes you get it wrong.

And perhaps in my attempt to write down their story I've gotten it wrong, I may have, but I don't think I'm that far off, it's not like I'm not used to using my head. I mean, sure, I'm not hardcore like my dad, even if Mette says he's not all that hardcore, that it's all his hermeneutics, all his intuition and all his sensory abilities. For rocks. Weird guy, I say. Mette thinks he's a great scientist, precisely because he combines the hard natural sciences and the soft humanist ones, that's what she says, she says he's in touch with both his masculine and feminine sides. Fuck you, Mette.

And then we get into an argument, Mette and I. Mette wants me to be more manly. She'd rather see me as some kind of Doctor Livingstone or, well, a Clemens Carlsen – some kind of devil-may-care man who'd go to the ends of the earth – then I ask her where the hell a goddamn seminarian is supposed to go, and then she grins, Mette does, and nods upward.

I *did* actually try, I studied geology and math, but then I ended up completely breaking my father's heart. "Theology?" he said, "but that's not a science, that's sheer guesswork." So I asked him, "Doesn't your work also include a fair amount of guesswork?" but he swore it didn't, "Certainly not!" There was a huge difference. He didn't guess, he *sensed*.

Not that I'm some stalwart of the faith either. "You're an inquiring soul," Mette says. When she's feeling generous.

❧ When Clemens was sixteen, his father, Thorkild – who had a degree in agriculture – applied for a job in Viborg as a teacher at Asmildkloster Agricultural Institute, where he later went on to become president. He got the job and gave his notice at the Royal Veterinary and Agricultural College, where he had been working. The family moved from Frederiksberg to Viborg, and Clemens started tenth grade at Cathedral High School.

In a new pair of knickers whose soft folds hung down to the middle of his shins, he crossed the school courtyard, pushed open the door, and walked up the dark, varnished stairs until he was standing in front of his new classroom.

He carefully opened the door and went in. The room was empty. But the pungent odour of sweat and formaldehyde accosted his nostrils, and he scurried across the floor to the windows, which he flung open one by one. Along the walls hung glass cabinets containing preserved grass snakes, a rigid fox, a ferret frozen in mid-jump, and a badger that was just about to catch a mouse. A large map of Denmark covered much of the wall behind the teacher's desk.

Clemens walked over to it and let his finger slide down through Jutland, over the Little Belt Bridge, across the Great Belt, and over Zealand until it reached Copenhagen. Suddenly the map rolled up, revealing a chalkboard covered with chalk marks. Clemens took a step back and tilted his head to the side so he could make sense of the marks he was seeing. There was a cock rising out from between two round balls in the middle of the board, and propped on top of that the lower half of a woman with an enormous ass and a tiny waist. In another spot there was a pair of breasts with huge, hard nipples protruding from the top of a dress.

Clemens heard someone clear her throat. There was a woman leaning against the doorframe. Lightning fast he turned his back to her, stuck his hand down into his pants and adjusted his hardon upward so it was pointing straight at his belly button. Almost hidden behind his fly. Then he turned to face the woman, who was still standing in the doorway. She smiled. He felt the heat surge down through his body and thought this was how she would always picture him. Blushing, his fly brimming.

She walked over to him, but he didn't see her. He saw only himself, standing there, his face red and his eyes burning with shame. If only he hadn't looked away. If only he'd looked her straight in the eye. Then she wouldn't have seen his shame.

"Hi," she said. "I'm Miss Brandt, and you must be Clemens Carlsen."

Clemens didn't hear what she said. Miss Brandt held out her hand to him, and he took it.

"Hi," he whispered, seeing only her hand.

She twisted it free and set it on the desk next to them.

"This is your seat," she said.

Clemens nodded and sat down.

A moment later girls and boys streamed into the room, their voices loud because the bell hadn't rung yet. A skinny boy who looked like one of the weak-chested kids Clemens had seen when his mother was staying at the Sanatorium on Vejle Fjord slid onto the bench next to him.

"Hi! I'm Mini," he said, holding his bony hand out to Clemens.

"Mini?" Clemens said, grasping his hand.

"Well, my real name is Ernst," Mini said.

Clemens nodded.

"But here they call me Mini."

Clemens nodded again.

"I'm Clemens," he said. "That's my real name, too."

"Obviously."

There was a bang. Clemens looked up. The teacher was sitting behind her desk with the pointer in her hand.

"All right, settle down!" she said.

The room got a little quieter.

"Ole," she said nodding back toward the chalkboard, "clean that off!"

Mini started giggling and plunging his right index finger in and out of a hole he made using the thumb and index finger on his left hand. The teacher leaned back in her chair and crossed her arms.

"I suppose you all thought you could shock me with that," she said, shaking her head.

"What's her name?" Clemens whispered.

"Miss Brandt," Mini answered. "Her first name is Ane. Do you have a condom?"

Clemens wrinkled his brow.

"I'm going to come soon," Mini moaned while he plunged his index finger back and forth faster and faster.

"What class does she teach?"

"German," Mini moaned before flinging himself back against the backrest.

Miss Brandt leaned over her desk and started watching Mini closely. She didn't say anything and finally he slid down under his desk.

VIBORG, FEBRUARY 1942

ক Clemens pushed open the door to the stairwell of the building on Sankt Leonis Stræde and slowly shuffled up the stairs. It was his German translation. He hadn't gotten it done and Miss Brandt had insisted that he turn it in by that afternoon.

Mini had thrust his tongue back and forth in his cheek and whipped his index finger in and out of the hole that he pretty much always made with the thumb and index finger on his left hand.

"Well?" he insinuated.

"Shut up, you baboon," Clemens responded, shoving him in the chest so he had to take a step backward.

Mini was so small, and Clemens was pretty big.

Clemens had to knock several times before Miss Brandt opened the door.

"Oh, it's you," she said, already on her way back into the apartment again.

Clemens hesitated in the doorway, but then followed. She was already gone and he was standing in the living room with his composition book in his hand.

"Just make yourself comfortable. Go ahead and take your things off and set them on one of those chairs," she called from somewhere.

Clemens didn't respond.

"Hello? Are you there?" she called, sticking her head back in.

"Um, do you want me to take my clothes off?" he said.

"Yes, but just your coat and your scarf," she said with a smile.

But then she was already gone again.

13

Clemens was hot, and the hand that was holding his composition book was starting to feel clammy. He took off his coat and scarf and laid them over the back of the chair. He kept clutching the composition book.

Then she came in with a tray with a teapot and two cups and a little creamer of milk.

"Just put that on the table," she said, nodding at the book.

Clemens did what she asked.

"Do you take sugar?" she asked, raising her eyebrows.

Clemens shook his head. Mostly he just wanted to grab his coat and run out the door. But Miss Brandt was calm. As if Clemens were a guest and not a high school student with a German translation.

She pushed aside the books and stacks of homework and set out the cups and the teapot. The fabric of her dress hugged her hips tightly as she bent forward.

"Please," she said, gesturing that he should have a seat.

Then she poured the tea. Clemens became aware of his shirt sticking to his back and wondered if he should take off his sweater. But surely he had sweat rings under his arms.

Miss Brandt talked almost nonstop. Not restlessly, but resolutely.

"You're awfully quiet," she paused, smiling at him.

He looked down.

"It's OK," she said, reassuring him.

Then she grinned.

"Maybe that's what makes you seem more mature than the others. That and the fact that you're taller."

She nodded toward a point somewhere in the middle of his torso.

Clemens leaned in over the table and took a sip of tea. It suffused his mouth, soft and warm.

"Do you like living in Viborg?" she asked.

Clemens shrugged.

"I don't know," he said. "Everything is so small here."

He smiled and added, "And people talk funny."

She threw her head back, laughing.

Clemens looked at her throat. Then he stood up. Miss Brandt looked at him in surprise.

"I have to go now," he said.

She nodded and stood up as well. Suddenly she seemed a little flustered. Clemens felt calmer, and he looked down at her. If he reached out with his hand, he could touch her breast.

She held out her hand, and he shook it, averting his eyes, before bounding away down the stairs.

🙠 Anna and Clemens reached El-Khârga late in the day. The town rose up from the sand like an enormous beehive of rectangular, flat-roofed buildings that seemed to grow in and out of each other. Anna imagined that enormous fingers had dragged through the crust of the desert, modeling this tangled clump of buildings out of the excess sand.

The town stood with its back to the desert. There wasn't a single window penetrating its clay walls. There were only peepholes facing the courtyards, where the khamsin wind couldn't really get hold of the sand. The alleys, which weren't much wider than an arm's length, were covered with masonry or canvas so the sun and sand couldn't get to the people and animals below.

Outside of town the date palms stretched upward as if they were trying to scrape away the milky veil from the sky to get to the piercing blue colour that the desert sky reveals only in the winter.

Clemens and Anna parked the Jeep just outside El-Khârga. Then they walked into the alleys, into a world of darkness and muffled noises. A flock of boys followed them at a distance as they weaved haphazardly through town. It was impossible to keep track of where they were because there were so many passageways, and the sun wasn't visible anywhere so they couldn't use it to get their bearings. And Clemens was astonished at how the boys raced through the alleys so nimbly, as if navigating this underworld maze were the easiest thing you could imagine. As if they navigated using signs and markers he couldn't see or interpret.

A female form turned a corner up ahead. A hand protruded from the black material to support the jug she was carrying on her head. Otherwise the only things not covered were her safflower-painted eyes. Rocking back and forth, a man riding a donkey – which had such short legs that the man's

15

feet were almost dragging on the compacted sand – emerged from one passageway and vanished into another. An old man with glistening, white eyes and toothless gums toiled past them on two mismatched crutches.

The scent of cinnamon, coriander, and cardamom, and the stench of manure from animals and human excrement followed them, just like the boys through the labyrinth. Suddenly there was a new aroma, the scent of baking bread. It completely engulfed them, and Anna looked up and noticed a woman squatting in front of a dome-shaped oven on the flat roof above them. She covered her face with a corner of the black fabric enveloping her body. Five men were sitting farther off playing shish bish by the entrance to a bar. Several people were sitting in the darkness behind them around hookahs, smoking *margannana*. The men eyed Anna. She looked away. Clemens nodded and said hi.

Typical sounds of disapproval slid out of the bar with the smoke. Like a snake. There was a woman's voice. And with it various drum sounds. Some deep and cavernous as if they came from inside one of the desert's wells. Others regular and muffled. They were men's sounds, Anna thought, feeling her blood drain away like scalding water beneath her skin. She turned around to face the men at the bar, but Clemens pulled her along. So she turned around and followed him.

She started running.

"Anna?" Clemens yelled behind her.

She suddenly stopped.

"Listen!" she said.

"What?"

She raised her hand. Her eyes were closed.

The muezzin's voice filtered through the alleys, flowing over every single nook and bump in the clay walls. Up and down. In and out. Like a Tuareg's hands between a woman's thighs. Like salt caravans moving over knurled Seif dunes, their sandy ridges exposed to the ice-cold desert night.

Anna started to hum. Cautiously and hesitantly she formed her lips around the notes. At first they sounded European. Then in an Arab style, they alternated between half tone and three-quarter tone intervals. Sounding sentimental and sorrowful, Clemens thought.

Anna and Clemens followed the sound and it wasn't long before they reached a small square in front of a mosque. The minaret rose over the houses, and the muezzin stood way up under the onion-shaped crown singing out over the desert.

After giving a boy a few piastres to show them the way they finally found the Trans-Saharan Hotel on the outskirts of El-Khârga. It turned out they could have gotten there by driving around the outside of the town.

The hotel was an arbitrary mix of a bare-bones Arab inn and one of those British hotels in Luxor or Cairo. It wasn't fancy, but it was still a vast improvement over the one in Asyût.

Anna was shown up to a room with an old, polished double bed and a triple mirror while Clemens went back for the Jeep. She set her satchel on the bed and sat down. The plaster around the ceiling light was cracked, and in some places it had flaked off in big pieces.

Someone was walking out in the hallway. Anna had a sinking feeling in her stomach. The footsteps were heavy. And every now and then they stopped. Anna got up. She longed for Clemens. She wanted to hear his boots out there. Bounding up the stairs. But surely it would take him a little while longer. Maybe a long time. He might get lost in those alleys. Go the wrong way. He might get really lost. Anna sat down on the bed. Clemens should go around the city. Along the wall. Then he wouldn't get lost, then he would get to the Jeep without having to go through the labyrinth. That's what he should do. Oh, she should have told him that. That he should go around the outside. She opened her bag and fished out a piece of paper. It was the Anna Blossom poem that Clemens had written out for her a long time ago. She unfolded it and pushed it in under the frame of the mirror. Up in the left-hand corner.

It took a really long time. When she finally heard his footsteps, the knot in her stomach burst and the warmth from it spread to every single cell.

"You have to stop being so scared, Anna," he said, pulling her head in against his chest.

VIBORG, MARCH 1943

ॐ Clemens rested his chin on his hand. It wasn't raining, but the air was heavy with the damp. It was dripping from the trees and eaves; at any moment the air particles might become saturated, become so full of moisture they had to overflow. Not as rain, but moisture oozing out of plain air. That's what Clemens was thinking before he sighed and turned his attention to the teacher.

They were well into their junior year. Miss Brandt was writing on the board in her ugly, almost illegible scrawl. She was writing German verbs. Clemens mouthed the words with his lips, but quickly drifted back out into the watery coldness. Two German soldiers walked by out on Sankt Olufsbakke. The soldiers had stopped a man who had been hurrying away, his shoulders hunched and his cap drenched. He fumbled for his papers in a breast pocket under his sweater. Once they had looked at them, he was allowed to proceed and disappeared down Ålborgvej. The Germans disappeared too, but a few minutes later a shot rang out. Clemens jumped and he looked up at Miss Brandt who had frozen mid-motion up by the board. A pained look swept over her face, and her eyes sought out Clemens, who was already looking at her. The others cried out and rushed over to the windows, but Clemens stayed seated, and Miss Brandt went on looking straight into his eyes. He could see that something resembling grief was welling up in her, and he tried to give her a smile. Warmly and almost imperceptibly. She blushed, down along her throat and over the part of her breasts he could see above the neckline of her blouse.

Then abruptly she turned toward the windows.

"Back to your seats," she said loudly.

But her eyes drifted back to Clemens. Something fell into place. He wasn't smiling anymore now, but he kept looking at her. Even though he was only seventeen and should have been afraid and self-conscious.

Miss Brandt returned to the verbs on the board, but was interrupted by Ole, who was tilting his chair back.

"To hell with German!" he said.

Miss Brandt turned around, raising her eyebrows.

"I can't even fucking stand to listen to that Kraut talk," he continued.

She set the chalk down on her desk and walked around her desk to where the students' seats started.

"Now listen up, Ole," she said. "I understand your anger. We all feel it. But there are some rules and we have to follow them. And if you want to graduate from high school, you are going to have to pass your German exam."

"But, sheesh, we can't even stand to listen to that crappy language," Jacob chimed in.

Miss Brandt leaned forward over her desk. Then she took a deep breath.

"I understand that," she said quietly. "Really I do. But remember, the more you know, the stronger you are. For example, don't you think the British need people who can speak German? If you can understand the enemy, it's easier to defeat them."

She looked around the room. Ole was sitting there drumming on the desk with his pencil. Clemens was leaning back, looking up at her. She turned around and rearranged two pieces of chalk in the chalkrail below the blackboard. Then she started walking around the room.

"And, of course, there are other Germans besides the ones who are running around out there right now," she said, nodding toward the windows. "Great philosophers and poets. Goethe and Rilke, for example. Rilke taught himself Danish just so he could read Jens Peter Jacobsen. That's how much someone can love language and literature. And Kurt Schwitters, he's anything but what you associate with German: his poems are crazy, full of chaos and love. He…"

But then the bell rang, and she stopped her wandering and stood still. Everyone teemed out except Clemens who stayed seated, his back to her. Soon everyone was out of the classroom and only the two of them were left. He didn't turn around, and she didn't walk over to him. But after a moment she started walking after all. She stopped right in front of him and turned him around so she could look down into his face.

"OK," she almost whispered. "I'll be home at three."

She turned around and took a step forward, but then stopped. Clemens stood up, took his schoolbag and walked past her. Very slowly. And she was looking right at his throat. Then he slipped out of the classroom.

At three o'clock he stood outside her door. His blood was seething, it hurt beneath his skin. She had changed her clothes, and the coffee-brown sweater she wore now fit snugly and followed the curve of her breasts. She had big breasts. That was one of the first things he had noticed. Other than her mouth, which was sultry and pulled a little crookedly to the one side. He had dwelled on what it would be like in that mouth. How it would feel to stick a finger in there and let it slide over the wetness behind her lower lip and then all the way in to the tongue in the middle. Into where it was warmest of all.

She stepped aside and let him in.

"Ah, it's you," she said.

That was it, then she walked back to the kitchen. Clemens stood there for a bit and noticed the noise inside his head. This fizzing. Then he draped his coat over the back of the chair. Everything in her living room seemed drawn with an unnatural crispness and precision, like rocks and trees on an October day.

A clinking sound came from the kitchen. A cupboard door opened and closed, cups rattled against each other, and water spurted out of the faucet. Then there was silence. He listened and waited for more sounds, but there weren't any.

Clemens went back there. On the table was a tray with cups and a creamer. The teapot was sitting next to the tray. It was open, the lid was sitting in back of it. She was standing in front of the sink with her back to Clemens. The noise in his head started again, and he felt dizzy and stopped in the middle of the floor. She didn't move. She was a fossil. But then she bent her neck, and the light from outside fell on her skin and brought it to life. He reached out his hand and let his fingers touch the skin just there. His cock, which had been throbbing, radiating heat since he had left Cathedral High School, now rose hard as stone, and she arched her neck as if she were following his fingers as they slid down over her skin. Then she turned around. Clemens tried to inhale, to pull the air all the way down to his stomach, but couldn't. It was stuck, quivering in his chest. She looked at him. Her mouth was sultrier than usual, loose and half open. But the look in her eyes was intense. Desire was on top, behind that a pent-up desperation, and in the very back shame.

"Oh, you…" she whispered. "I'm *too* old."

Clemens could feel her breasts, and his skin was aching again. So when she put her hand on the back of his head and pressed his face down toward hers, it hurt.

She lifted her face up to his. Her face was sincere. Her eyes were almost closed, but not so much that he couldn't sense how she was looking out from somewhere in there.

Late in the afternoon they were lying in her bed. The bedroom was full of books Clemens hadn't even noticed. He glanced around.

"You read a lot?" he asked.

She was lying on her stomach with one arm in over his chest.

"It's very wrong, what we've done," she said, rolling over onto her back.

Clemens didn't respond.

"If only it had been your father," she said. "That would have been better."

Clemens frowned.

"You look a lot like him, actually," she said. "You're both good-looking men. Although strictly speaking I suppose you're not quite a man yet."

Clemens snorted.

"You're damn right I'm a man! I'll be eighteen soon."

It was precisely this mixture of boyhood and manhood that Ane found alluring. The boyishness made the man in him stand out more clearly. To her, Clemens was more of a man than any man who had thoroughly given up boyish things.

And yet he still had a boisterous youthful pulse under his skin. His desire for her was foremost in his gaze, and because he apparently had no idea how obvious it was, he never tried to hide it. There was never a time when she would look into his eyes without encountering that uncontrollable lust that sent all the blood in her body instantly gushing down to the folds of her labia.

But although the need in his eyes was more demanding than in most grown men's, she could plant the seeds of confusion in him effortlessly. Then he would furrow his brow, as though withdrawing into himself, as though trying to understand what had happened. What had changed to cause this different sensation in him. And in this way she could force him to vacillate between desire and confusion.

  From the terrace on the roof of the hotel you could look out over the desert. The flat land stretched out to the east with scattered scrub plants over by the Nile Valley. To the west, furrowed, dry valleys pulled the salty desert crust downwards, puckered it into wrinkles like chapped skin, and left a scarred landscape of principal and tributary valleys. Like a river system. And at one time there had been water here too. Water that had rushed over the red earth to flow out into the Nile a hundred kilometres farther to the east.

"When are the others arriving?" Anna asked.

"Not until tomorrow afternoon."

In the evening sun, Clemens's nose cast a shadow over the left half of his face. Just as the low outcroppings cast black copies of themselves against the sedimentary mountains behind them. He pulled his shoulders up to protect himself from the chill that was setting in and turned toward Anna.

She was leaning against the balustrade of the rooftop terrace, and Clemens let one finger glide over her taut back.

The darkness was dense now, and Anna had gone back downstairs a long time ago. Clemens tipped his head back and tried to identify constellations. There was one whose name he couldn't remember and that was bugging him, but it was cold and he was freezing. With his hands sunk deep in his pockets and his shoulders hunched up, he left the roof terrace and went back down. He took his boots off before slipping in the door to his and Anna's room. Even from the doorway, he could hear Anna's heavy breathing, meaning she was asleep. A cockroach crawled across the strip of light that pierced the room from the half-open door. Clemens knelt down and squashed the critter with his boot as noiselessly as possible. He tossed it out the door and then shut it carefully. Anna rolled over but was still asleep. In the moonlight shining through the high-set windows, too high for anyone to be able to look out, he could make out her hip as she lay there on her side with the blanket over her. They'd gotten wider, her hips, in the time they'd known each other. He squatted next to her, pulled the blanket down a little and brought his face closer to her hip. Then he let his lips follow the curve from her thigh up over her hip and down to her waist. She stirred and he pulled off her underwear.

Anna was half asleep and half awake, he could see that. And he could also see that that's where she wanted to be. She didn't want to wake up. She wanted to doze and feel heavy and unfurl for him. He knew her and knew that's what she wanted to do.

She spread her thighs for him so his hands could glide along the smooth skin on the insides of her thighs until they came together at her vulva. Then she put one leg around the back of his neck and with both hands she pulled his face down against her. He smiled. It was a demand. That's how she was, his Anna.

The next day they were drinking tea up on the hotel's roof terrace, under the greyish white sailcloth. Every now and then the wind would whip the material aside and they would have to squint so they wouldn't get sand in their eyes. Suddenly the sound of a car horn swept up over the balustrade along with the sand. Anna went over and peered down at the packed car that had pulled up in front of the hotel. The equipment on the roof was covered with a brown tarp.

A flock of boys in white, ankle-length galabeyas was thronging around the two men who had just gotten out of the car. Two of the boys started scrambling onto the roof of the car, and one of the men had time only to wave his hand dismissively and yell something at them when the first suitcase was hauled from under the tarp and tossed onto the ground. The second man put his hand up to shield his eyes from the sun; he glanced up toward Anna and started waving. She withdrew.

"They're here," she said.

Clemens closed his books and his little notepad and tucked them under his arm.

The children had scurried into the lobby of the hotel. The men towered over the black froth of boys' hair, one a little shorter and stockier than the other, but both of them wearing sand-coloured shorts, sweaty off-white shirts and white cloths wrapped as poorly fashioned turbans over their dusty faces.

By the time Anna and Clemens made it down there, the stockier of the men emerged from the sea of boys, extended one hand to Clemens, and clapped him on the upper arm with his other.

"Great to see you again, Clemens," he said, smiling broadly.

"Hello, Leo," Clemens said. "I hope the trip went well?"

Then he turned toward Anna.

"This is Anna. My wife," he said.

Leo grasped her hand and gave it a light kiss as he bent his head.

"Even though we're teetering on the edge of civilization, surely we can still maintain a modicum of social grace," he said.

"On the way into the wilderness people always cling so desperately to their civilized masks," the other man said. "But it doesn't take many days until the wind starts tearing and pulling them apart at the seams. I've seen lots of men with their masks dangling by one last, crumbling thread."

Leo turned around and made a sweeping gesture with his arm.

"Please allow me to introduce Peter," he said. "Who always – how should I put it? – always looks on the bright side of life."

Clemens smiled, and Anna grinned, holding her hand out to the tall man.

"I've been looking forward to meeting you," Peter said, a tinge of bashfulness in his voice.

His eyes were mismatched; one was larger than the other and dismissive to the point of seeming angy. The other was narrow, kind of squinted shut, as if he were winking all the time. To apologize for the angry one.

An hour later Clemens pulled the black cloth aside to let the others enter. The sand had formed miniature dunes over the trampled floor and under the six tables that stood along the wall. Two men were sitting at one of the tables, eating. One young and one old. Both wearing fezzes pulled down over their shiny black hair, their thighs spread wide under their galabeyas. They didn't take their eyes off the newcomers who had just walked in.

"Are you here to eat?" asked a girl who entered the room through a door in the corner.

"Yes, thank you," Clemens answered.

The girl indicated a table and they sat down. Anna next to Clemens. He rested one of his hands on his knee and Anna laid hers on top of it.

"We have soup with lamb," the girl said.

Leo frowned.

"Do you have anything else?" he asked.

"We have dates. You can have that afterwards," the girl answered, looking off to the side and down at the floor.

"We'll take soup for four then," Peter said.

The girl nodded and turned around.

A little later a thickset man with oily skin came through the door. He was balancing four bowls full of soup and a basket of pita bread made with whole wheat flour. They ripped off pieces of the tough bread, letting them soak until they were sopping and heavy with soup before bringing them up to their lips.

A few hours later, the proprietor turned on the music, and the thickset man called his women out from the backroom and tied long handkerchiefs around their hips. The girl who had taken their order, a slightly older girl, and three adult women. With their arms raised and hands like snakes in front of their covered faces, they started swirling their accentuated hips in vibrating, circular motions.

The place was full now, and men were clapping in time to the rhythm. Some of the men clapped in a syncopated fashion, forming a counter rhythm to the beat. Without any attempt to hide it, the men all kept their eyes fixed on the women's quivering buttocks.

"Arab men are obsessed with women," Leo said. "You can see why the women are forced to keep themselves covered."

"Or maybe it's because the women cover themselves that the men get obsessed," Clemens said. "We'll never know the answer to that one."

"And you people call yourselves scientists?" Anna asked, putting down her glass. "Well, there's a failure to appreciate the value of the scientific method if ever I heard one! All you have to do is find the right method, and you'll be able to tell which causes which."

She leaned back and eyed the three men expectantly. Clemens ran his fingers playfully through her hair.

"Ah, that you could be so naïve," he said.

"She's not naïve," Leo cut in. "What good are we if we can't figure out how things affect each other? If we can't figure out cause and effect?"

He turned inquiringly to Peter, who was sitting there rolling a cigarette between his bony fingers.

"Long live positivism," he said. "I didn't know you were such a hard-nosed positivist, Leo. You and your constant whistling."

Anna started to grin.

"What does he whistle?" she asked.

"Sinatra," Leo said, grinning as well.

"All we can do is observe things that happen," Clemens said. "When you get right down to it, we can't prove what the underlying cause was. Take geological processes, for example. We can never know for sure what happened every step of the way. All we can do is reason out what may have happened. Or perhaps it will simply come to us in a burst of inspiration. Like with Wegener and continental drift – after studying a map, he suddenly realized that the east coast of South America fits into the west coast of Africa. Just the way a woman who's lying on her side fits perfectly into a man's body when he's lying behind her."

Leo laughed deeply and looked over at Anna.

"I mean," Clemens continued, "you can only bring these continents together in your mind."

"And a man and a woman can only be brought together in the mind?" Peter mumbled.

"Continental drift can never be proved, but we believe it all the same," Clemens continued. "At least some of us do."

"Yes, and some believe in God," Anna said.

"We can't prove the existence of God or continental drift, but there's a lot more circumstantial evidence to support the theory of continental drift than the theory of God," Clemens said.

"Well!" Leo said, edging forward in his chair. "Let's not pull man and woman any farther apart from each other than we have to. It's enough that Africa and South America aren't connected anymore; a lot of people have lost their lives crossing the ocean to get from the one continent to the other."

☙ *"I drizzle your name."*

Ane stopped reading to chuckle, then continued, *"Anna Blossom, You drippy beast, I – love – your!"* She read in her deep voice. A little surprised. "Your?" she said, looking straight ahead. "Your?"

"Huh?" Clemens said from the bed.

Ane was sitting at her desk. Naked. The window above the desk was all fogged up.

"'I love your,' Clemens?" she said, shaking her head.

"Huh? What are you talking about?" he repeated.

"It's Kurt Schwitters. A love poem," Ane explains.

"It sounds weird," Clemens said, sliding his leg down onto the floor. "Very, um, modern."

"It is. Even though it was written twenty-two years ago. Shall I read some of it to you?"

She looked over at him. He nodded, preparing to listen, resting his hands behind his head and closing his eyes.

"A – N – N – A! I drizzle your name.
Your name drips like tallow.
Do you, Anna, you do know,
People can also read you from behind."

Clemens chuckled from the bed.

"And you, the most splendid of all,
You are from behind as from in front: A – N – N – A.
CARESSING drizzles tallow over my back.
Anna Blossom, you drippy beast,
I – love – your!"

27

Ane set the book down, running her eyes over Clemens. "Crazy, isn't it?" she said.

He smiled suggestively and pulled the comforter aside. "E – N – A, come over here," he said. "I want to read you from behind."

She chuckled. And got up from the chair.

They spent most of their time in that bedroom. In that bed.

"You should have a woman who's firmer," she said.

"Don't start that again!" he said.

"Well, it's true," she said. "Someone whose breasts don't slide off to the side when she lies down."

"But that's exactly what I like," he said.

"You're weird," she said. "Eighteen-year-olds are totally into that kind of thing. They want firm, young girls."

"Really?" he asked. "Is that what they want?"

"Yes," she said.

"Do you know what an eighteen-year-old really wants?" he asked.

"No."

"To be able to walk around in public with his girlfriend."

She sighed, sitting up in the bed.

"You're ashamed of me!" he complained.

"No, Clemens," she chided. "I'm not ashamed of you!"

He looked at her.

"Yes, you are!"

She hit the mattress with her hand.

"No, I'm not!" she insisted. "Actually, I'm proud of you. I'm proud that a handsome young man like you would want an old lady like me."

She sighed.

"But Viborg is a really small town."

"Screw that!"

"Perhaps you don't have as much to lose as I do," she said. "I could lose my job."

Clemens got up, reaching for his underwear on the chair.

"And what do you think your parents would say?" she asked.

Clemens thought about it. Then he smiled.

"I bet my father would be a little envious."

She tried to smile, but didn't quite pull it off.

"Maybe it's *me* I'm ashamed of," she said.

Clemens was standing in the middle of the floor. He'd gotten his underwear on.

"If you're ashamed of yourself, then you're ashamed of me too," he said.

She frowned.

"Otherwise there wouldn't be any reason for you to feel ashamed of yourself, now, would there?" he said.

"Just hold it right there," she said, her eyebrows shooting upward. "What are you saying?"

"I'm just saying that you wouldn't have any reason to feel ashamed of yourself if there weren't some reason for you to be ashamed of me. That's all."

He seemed impatient.

"I've always known that those cogs spin around pretty fast up there," she said, pointing at his forehead. "It's starting to get late now, and I'm a little tired."

She laughed slightly. Very slightly. If anything, it was a smile with sound added to it.

Then she said, "No, you listen to me. I'm not ashamed because there's any reason to be ashamed of *you*. I'm ashamed of myself because…"

She took a deep breath trying to think of how to put it into words. It worried her that he was standing there seeming so impatient and recalcitrant.

"I'm ashamed because a grown woman like me shouldn't be interested in boys who are almost young enough for me to be their mother."

"Well, you would have had to get started really early for that," he said.

"Sixteen," she said. "A lot of people become mothers when they're sixteen."

"Well, not a *lot*," he said.

"Some," she said.

She pulled the comforter up around her shoulders.

"No, I just mean," she continued, "that people would think all kinds of things about *me*. About *you* I'm sure they would just think that you're quite the Casanova. But *me*…"

"So, what are they going to think about you?"

"Well, that I…"

She shook her head and thought for a moment.

"That I'm a slut or something. That I'm leading you astray. That here's this sweet little boy and then there's this mother figure who just has her way with him, taking advantage of his innocence."

He laughed and flung his arms out.

"And what difference would that make?" he exclaimed. "What the fuck does it matter what they think or don't think… You know what?"

She shook her head.

"They don't think worth *shit*! Because they don't fucking have anything to think with!"

She laughed, and he looked down at her, smiling.

"Stupid little podunk town!" he said.

And then he started laughing too.

"Boy, are we grumpy!"

"Yeah, we sure are," she said. "But, seriously, do you miss Copenhagen?"

He nodded.

"I'm going back the day I finish high school," he said. "And you're coming with me!"

"Come here," she said, reaching out to him.

The next time he rang her doorbell, she was ready with her bag and cardigan, and she was wearing lipstick and had done her hair. He looked at her in surprise.

"What the hell?" he said.

"We're going out," she said.

He flung out his arms and hopped backward onto the stairs, his legs together.

"Wonderful!" he said. Then he stepped to the side and made a gentlemanly motion with his arm to invite her to go first.

She locked the door and walked past him. He bounded past her down the stairs until he stopped on the landing, where he waited for her. She smiled wryly, shaking her head.

"My Clemens!" she said.

"I like the sound of that," he said.

He thrust his hand into Ane's and intertwined his fingers with hers.

It was the middle of May and the evening was pleasantly warm. They walked down to Borgvold Park and strolled around a little looking at the flowers and the kayakers out on Lake Nørre.

"Someday I hope to see you scooting around in a kayak," she said.

"That can easily be arranged if you start going out with me."

Pairs of lovers sat on the benches, kissing or holding hands.

"Come on," Clemens said, pulling her over onto a free bench.

They sat down.

"Now we're sitting here like everyone else," he said, smiling.

෫ In the morning Leo went out to find them a cook. And Clemens and Anna tried to get some more gas.

Clemens asked at the reception desk and found out that there wasn't a single gas station in all of El-Khârga. But they could try at the depot in the alley behind the café. They had a little of everything there and surely they'd have gas too.

Anna and Clemens crisscrossed their way through the alleys and got lost several times, but they finally got there. In the dusty shop there were bolts of fabric, bundles of carpets, hurricane lamps and quite a bit of other stuff. Including kerosene and gasoline dispensed from a thirty litre barrel. But the gas was really low quality, so Clemens slipped a dollar into the palm of the shopkeeper who promised he'd be back that same afternoon with a couple of barrels of high octane gas from out by the airport in Bahr.

So they ended up having to stay in El-Khârga for another day.

Leo did succeed in finding a cook. His name was Sayeed. And after they loaded the high octane gas onto the roof of one of the Jeeps, they left the town and its covered alleys behind and drove out into the sun.

Anna and Clemens led the way, followed by Peter, Leo, and Sayeed in the second car. Peter drove, Sayeed sat in the middle, and Leo was hanging out the window on his side of the car. The sand was flying into his eyes and mouth, and he had to pull his head back in. A little later it popped back out again, wrapped up in a scarf, with just a slit for his eyes. Anna leaned out and grinned at him. He waved his whole arm at her. She could see Peter shaking his head from behind the wheel.

"He's quite a serious guy, that Peter," she said, looking at Clemens.

He shrugged.

"A grown-up," he said, smiling at her.

She pulled her harmonica out of the glove box and put it to her lips. It was full of sand which she had to blow out before the metal could form any notes.

Clemens caressed the back of her head, but she was far away now. He knew that. He only had her on borrowed time. For moments. But she was the most splendid woman he could imagine. She was his Anna Blossom.

They drove for two days before they reached the spot where their camp would be. Leo and Peter set up the tents while Clemens got the chests with the instruments and books and maps down from the roof of the Jeep and put them in the tent he and Anna would be sleeping in. Anna unfolded the cots, unrolled the sleeping bags, carried her satchel into their tent, and placed it under the bed. After that she helped Sayeed find the food.

Once the chests were down and he had set up the little table under the awning of the tent, Clemens got to work. He spread out the map that the cartographer had made on the expedition in 1956 and studied the meticulous markings denoting soil conditions. He slid one hand over the stippled lines that delineated the wadis, the greyish black splotches that indicated sedimentary mountains, and the yellow areas that suggested that here the soil was especially rich in sodium sulfate, common salt, or magnesium sulfate. In other places, salt lakes had been drawn in, formed by water evaporating from the arm of a lake that had been cut off from the sea at some point by geological changes. And then in other places the brown colouration meant that the desert had formed a brown crust there, composed of iron and manganese compounds.

Clemens set the compass on the map and wrote their position on his notepad. He jotted everything down here: the route of the expedition, descriptions of soil conditions, various rock formations, discoveries of fossils and flint concretions, things he wanted to remember and occasional diary entries.

↝ The snow lay in mounds along Toldbodgade as Clemens biked over to the garage on his way home to chat with Erling. The other assistants and apprentices weren't there. Erling was the only one there. And he was bending over a German car pouring grey powder into the oil fill hole.

"What the hell are you doing?" Clemens asked.

Erling winked at him.

"It's Carborundum," he said.

"No way. You're pulling my leg, man!" Clemens said.

Erling closed the hood and hid the sack in a corner behind some old tires.

"What does it do?" Clemens asked.

"The car can go about fifteen kilometres, then it dies," Erling said, drying his hands on a bundle of cotton rags.

"Do the others know about this?" Clemens asked.

Erling shook his head.

"You're pulling my leg, man," Clemens said again. "Are you part of some group then?"

"I kind of do this on my own."

"But you *are* part of a group? I bet you are, Erling!"

Erling turned around and walked across the garage. Clemens followed him.

"What kind of group is it?" he asked.

Erling stopped by the pit. There was a pack of cigarettes down there. He jumped down to get it.

Clemens squatted by the edge.

"What do you do?" he asked.

"Enough already, Clemens," Erling said, jumping up out of the pit and lighting a cigarette. He stuffed the pack into his chest pocket.

Clemens didn't say anything. With the toe of his boot he poked at a monkey wrench that was lying there on the floor. Then he looked up.

"You should know that you can trust me," he said.

Erling didn't respond. But then he nodded.

"I know I can," he said.

Both Lake Nørre and Lake Sønder were frozen over the following Sunday, so instead of going down to the kayak club, Erling and Clemens walked over to Cathedral High School. They managed to coax the window of the gym open and crawl in and then down the wall bars. It smelled dank and musty in there, but there was tons of space and they pulled out the climbing ropes and started climbing up them.

Clemens felt the heat prickling under his skin and took off his shirt. Erling could do back handsprings, and he was thumping his way diagonally across the floor. Clemens couldn't do those. He walked on his hands. Around and around.

"You gotta fucking learn how to do this!" Erling said, coming over to him.

Clemens dropped back down onto his feet.

"I don't know," he said.

"Just come on. I'll teach you."

Clemens smiled. His hair was sticking to his forehead and a shiny film of sweat covered his chest.

"Stand with your back to me," Erling said, "and then just go full force over backward. I'll support you."

Clemens pushed off but toppled over sideways.

"You need a lot more energy in it. You have to believe it!"

Clemens nodded, squatted down on his knees and tensed every muscle in his massive body until he leaped backward releasing all the energy he'd compressed. He felt Erling's hand supporting the small of his back, but he had too much speed and wasn't able to get his footing when he landed. But he did make it all the way around.

Erling clapped him on the shoulder.

"Good, now you've almost got it," he said. "Now all you have to do is just land on your feet."

Clemens nodded concentrating all his attention and strength on the jump, and this time he came around and landed on his feet.

A huge smile spread across his face before he lunged forward, jumping up on Erling, who tumbled over backward.

ᔕ

Clemens ran out to the equipment room to get the vaulting horse when he discovered that the door to the girls' locker room was open. He waved Erling over and disappeared into the dank room.

"Sheesh, this room smells just as rancid as the boys' locker room," Erling said when he walked in.

Clemens nodded. "But the boys' locker room doesn't have things like this hanging around in it," he said, taking a pair of panties down from a peg between two mirrors. He tossed them over to Erling who buried his whole face down into them.

"Mmm," he said, rolling his eyes so the whites showed before tossing them back to Clemens.

"Whose do you think they are?" Clemens mumbled before inhaling a whiff.

"Actually they don't really smell that good, but still they just make me so fucking horny," Erling said.

Clemens hung them back up.

"That would be the animal in us," he said, smiling.

Erling lay down on one of the enameled benches.

"How are things going with your teacher lady?" he asked.

"She reads me crazy poems," Clemens said, lying down on the bench so the soles of his feet were up against the soles of Erling's feet.

"She reads you poems?" Erling shook his head and said, "well, that's fucked up!"

Clemens laughed.

"I mean, we screw too if that's what you're wondering."

"I was about to get extremely worried about you."

Clemens put his hands behind his head and stared up at the flickering fluorescent light on the ceiling.

"Does she get all hot and heavy?"

"Yes. But that's all I'm going to say about that!"

"All right, dude."

The fluorescent went out, and the room got dark.

"Erling?" Clemens asked.

"Yes?"

"Let me join your group."

Erling didn't respond.

"Erling?"

"They'll say you're too young."

"The hell they will. I'm eighteen, and you're only twenty-one."

"I don't know. I can't just be dragging in any old guy I meet off the street."

"I'm not some fucking guy off the street. I'm Clemens. And just look how fast I learned to do a back handspring."

Erling laughed.

"It's really not up to me," he said.

"No, but, you know, you could ask."

Erling nodded.

"What?" Clemens prompted.

"I didn't say anything. I nodded."

Clemens leaped up.

"Awesome! Thanks, Erling!"

EL-KHÂRGA, NOVEMBER 1996

☙ I've got way too much time on my hands down here, I mean, sure, I'm making a lot of phone calls and sending a lot of e-mail and I'm always going to see Hamad, but there's still a lot of time left over, and I'm worried about them, my parents, so I can't really get any work done, I mean I *did* bring work along, but I can't concentrate, and I always end up sitting here writing and digging around in my mom and dad's papers and photographs from their expedition out into the Western Desert. In 1958.

I have a picture where they're standing in front of the Jeep, my mom's hair is stiff with all the sand and salt, she's grinning and looking off to the side somewhere in front of her, a little shyly, even though her body looks very steady and strong. She's standing next to Leo. He's pulled his hat down over his forehead and is peeking over at her from the shadow under its brim. Peter is standing behind my mother, to the side a little, watching Leo. He looks irritated, and my father is standing next to Peter and is the only one looking at the camera. His arms are crossed. Mette thinks he looks stern in the picture, I don't really know, calm and collected I would say, at any rate there's certainly no doubt that he's the one leading the expedition.

᷒ When it was dark and Sayeed had the food ready, they sat around the campfire and ate. A goulash of fava beans, small sinewy bits of goat meat, and millet flatbread to go with it. They drank beer too. And it didn't take long before they'd had enough for everyone to be in high spirits. The night air was filled with laughter and anecdotes concerning earlier expeditions: by Burton and Speke, Livingstone, Stanley, and especially Denmark's own Niebuhr back in the 1760s. And in the middle of all the tales Leo chimed in with his own stories of dehydration and snakebites that he told with a twinkle in his eyes and effusive arm gestures. He claimed to know why Burton and Speke had *really* argued about the source of the Nile south of them down in the heart of Africa or the *actual* reason why Samuel Baker and his Hungarian wife Florence never made it any further than Lake Albert in *their* quest for the source of the Nile.

Anna listened with interest and every now and then she would lean back, laughing genuinely, while Clemens followed Leo intensely with his eyes. He didn't say much. He might interject a "you don't say" or a skeptical "hmm" here or there, but otherwise he was quiet. Anna looked at him now and then, and when she did his eyes would move from Leo to her, but not otherwise. And as the evening wore on, Leo's stories grew more and more incoherent and edgy. And his eyes shifted toward Clemens more and more often.

"You're awfully young to be leading an expedition," he said suddenly, directing his comment to Clemens.

Clemens shrugged.

"You've always worked hard, haven't you, scrambling your way up the ladder of ambition?" Leo persisted. "High school, university, and now you're sitting here."

Clemens shook his head.

"Nah," he said.

"Nah?" Leo asked.

Clemens leaned forward and reached for a branch that had tumbled out of the campfire a little.

"Nah? What's that supposed to mean?"

"He was a mechanic," Anna said.

She wished Clemens would've said it himself. That he would talk and tell the others about himself.

"A mechanic?" Peter chimed in.

Clemens shrugged.

"I think it was something about a woman," Anna said.

Leo raised his eyebrows.

"Oh," he said. "Women. Have you had a lot of them, Clemens?"

"How many is a lot?" he responded.

Anna looked up at the sky and smiled, thrilled. She loved it when men talked about women. It was as if they were talking about her, as if they were actually sitting there talking about how much they desired her. Anna. The woman. As if they were picturing her naked body before them. In her mind she lay down naked before each one of them, one by one, and watched each man's eyes concentrating on taking in each part of her.

She enjoyed being the only woman here. The only one with four men in the middle of the desert. And she already felt like everything was revolving around her. She was the absolute centre of the group, the point where all of their energies converged.

"No, you would never want to just throw out a number!" Leo said, trying to smile.

He turned to Peter.

"What about you, Peter," he said. "Have you had many?"

Peter looked down and shook his head.

"I've never been that good at convincing them of what an excellent choice I am," he said. "Although, of course I am!"

Clemens smiled.

"And what makes you such an excellent choice, Peter?"

It was Leo who asked, and his voice had lightened again.

"I'm an excellent choice," Peter repeated and then paused.

Then he held up his hands.

"Because of these," he said. "These hands. Big and bony as they are, but you can fit a lot of woman into a hand like this. And they fit so nicely in them, women do. I mean once they come to appreciate them, that is."

It was as if only now Clemens woke up. As if he moved further into the circle.

"I believe that, Peter!" he said. In a vigorous voice.

Anna turned to look at Clemens. That was a trivial, boring thing to say, she thought. And to say with such authority, too. But Clemens liked Peter, the tall, clumsy stork of a guy with the bony hands. And that was probably the only way he could express it.

Peter reminded Clemens of Jens, whom he had met during the war. Jens, the bomb guy. Jens was the one who'd taught him everything there was to know about time pencils, detonators, and plastic explosives. Jens had the same solid expertise and the same self-effacing way of presenting it that Peter did; and then they had the same tall, bony body. And all the warmth Clemens had come to feel for Jens when they were sitting by Lake Nørre drinking the whisky Clemens had swiped from his father after Clemens had caught him in bed with his Ane, Clemens transferred all that warmth to Peter. And it gave him a sense of calm having him by his side. The kind of solidity that Peter had is what allowed people to survive in the desert.

∿ The first month he was in Erling's group, Clemens didn't have permission to do anything besides lug around an old ditto machine. From one apartment to another. And he didn't know anything. He couldn't even guess how big the group was, who was in charge, or who the others were. Erling was the only one he knew.

But in January 1944 he made it further in. Not because he had distinguished himself in any way, rather someone must have just had faith in him. And besides, the Germans had starting cracking down on saboteurs, and the Gestapo had dismantled several resistance groups. So Clemens had figured it would be a long time before he would really be in. But maybe the pressure from the Germans had increased the need for more people in the group.

At any rate, now he finally got to meet Jens and Ditlev. In a little apartment in a rear building on Store Sankt Mikkel Gade. He had been there before with the ditto machine, which was down in the cellar of Erling's building now. Jens was squatting with his back facing the room. He was wearing a dark rayon coat and a cloth cap. On the floor in front of him were packages and string and rags and a gas can.

Erling nudged Clemens further into the room and introduced him to the others. Ditlev stepped into the cone of light cast by the bulb in the ceiling and held out his hand. The skin on his face was leathery, and his neck was thick. Mostly he looked like one of the fishermen from Vejers out on the west coast of Jutland, Clemens thought.

Only now did Jens get up. He was tall and looked tough. His skin was stretched taut over his forehead, and a vein ran like a blue rhizome from the bridge of his nose to his hairline. He wasn't much older than Clemens.

"We got an air drop yesterday," he said, nodding back at the explosives in the corner.

Clemens nodded.

"Of course most of it is in our storage locations, but we have a little here," he said.

Ditlev was putting the parts on the table, and Jens was sorting them.

"Take these two here," Jens said, picking up two packages of explosive charges from the table. "These are plastic explosives. We get them from the RAF. Finest quality. PE2."

His fingers worked confidently, and in a matter of seconds he'd fastened the explosive charges together with a piece of insulating tape and connected them to a white fuse.

"That way they explode at the same time," he said without looking up from what he was doing with his fingers.

"Right," Clemens said. He was so tense and he was trying to memorize everything.

"And these here," Jens said, "these are the time pencils. In one end there's a little glass vial of acid."

He held one up so Clemens could see.

"When you squeeze the tube here on the outside, the vial breaks and the acid corrodes a small steel wire, which then releases a striker."

Clemens nodded.

"The striker hits a percussion cap, which transfers the priming impulse to the detonator."

Ditlev's hands rested on the table.

"They come with different time delays," Ditlev explained. "That one there is a ten-minute delay. You can tell from the black on the safety strip there."

He nodded toward the pencil in Jens's hands.

"There," Jens said, dropping his hands to his side. "Someone's going to get his ass fried!"

஧ This page must have been lying out in the sun for a long time, because the writing is pretty faded, but not so much that I can't read it easily. Not that it contains any earth shattering observations, but it's the first I have from the expedition in fifty-eight, it's from April, and it's my dad's, and at first glance it's completely insignificant, and yet it turns out that it says quite a bit about him, I think.

Finally the camp is set up, and we can get to work. I think the group will work well together; obviously there's a little fine-tuning to be done, a few rough corners to sand down, but I believe that they're good men.

And Anna seems to be thriving too. She smiles a lot with Leo. It's good for her. And maybe the fact that she's apparently found a new cheerfulness with Leo will get her to be present a little more. Here with the rest of us.

And then, of course, it's a phenomenal asset for the expedition to have a doctor along. That would certainly have spared some lives when we were in the Qattâra Depression in 1956.

CC, latitude 24° north, longitude 27° east. 1958

43

࿊ Thorkild was a good-looking man with broad shoulders and strong forearms jutting out of his shirtsleeves, which he always kept folded up to his elbows. He was a tad vain, and every morning he would slather his head with Brylcreem so that the hair clumped into glistening ropes that stretched from his brow back over his head. Now and then a tuft would flop loose and fall down to touch one of his cheekbones. Then Thorkild would run his big hand back through his hair, and the tuft would settle back into place between the others.

Thorkild met Clemens's mother for the first time in 1922. At the residence of the Danish government's sand dune inspector in Vejers. He had gone there to take a look at the rare plants that the inspector – flying in the face of all traditional knowledge and past experience – had managed to grow in the sandy, nutrient-poor soil just a few hundred metres inland from where the dunes started.

The dune inspector picked Thorkild up at the station in Oksbøl, and together they drove over the sand-strewn roads in the inspector's polished Opel over the heath and through the plantation to the dune inspector's residence. Rising from the earth where normally only stunted pine trees would grow, there was an expanse of beech trees, one after another, and they shimmered, their colours alternating between black and sandy, like a marble cake. The yard was surrounded by lilacs, and there were jasmine and honeysuckle encircling the patio. Even the king had visited this rare and exceptional garden. And now Thorkild was here. And, like the king, he had also come all the way from Copenhagen.

The dune inspector's wife was standing on the front steps when they pulled into the courtyard, but the instant the car came to a stop she turned and scurried off behind one of the outbuildings. The dune inspector cleared his throat and gave Thorkild a mighty thump on the back, signalling that they should make their way into the house. A strong floral scent hit Thorkild as he stepped into the entry hall with its low ceiling.

A girl took their blazers and hats, and the dune inspector showed Thorkild into the drawing room where a sumptuous spread of coffee and pastries had been laid out on a table in front of the door opening out onto the garden. There was a layer cake with chocolate icing on top and soft swathes of whipped cream around its sides. There were coconut cookies and *finskbrød* in glass seashell-shaped bowls, and resting on the blue, fluted cake plates there were neatly folded cloth napkins edged with cutwork embroidery.

"Please, help yourselves," the dune inspector said, gesturing toward the table with his arm.

"Thank you," Thorkild mumbled, pulling out a heavy mahogany chair, its seat embroidered with flowers.

The girl poured the coffee and sliced the layer cake. And it wasn't until Thorkild put the first spoonful of spongy cake to his lips that he noticed the young woman sitting at the other end of the room watching him.

He jumped.

"Martha!" the dune inspector said in his somewhat gruff voice, "come here."

Martha rose slowly. She wasn't particularly tall, and she was very thin. The skin on her face was pale beneath her dark hair that was pulled into a thick braid that hung down her back. Her eyes were brown and a bit deep-set. There was a peculiar listlessness to her face. Her lips were firm, her eyebrows motionless, and not even a twitch moved across her cheeks. But her eyes were restless. Almost wary. And every now and then the one eye would quiver in an uncontrollable tic that she tried to hide by turning that side of her face away.

Thorkild stood up holding out his hand to her. She glanced down and lifted hers, but not enough for it to reach all the way up to his. He gathered it up and gave it a gentle squeeze. Her hand was ice cold.

"Thorkild Carlsen," he said.

Martha nodded, but didn't say anything, and when Thorkild let go of her hand, she disappeared back to her spot at the very end of the drawing room. Almost hidden behind the grand piano.

The dune inspector sighed. And Thorkild marveled that the sap and vitality evident everywhere in the plants growing on the grounds here seemed to be completely absent from the women. One would almost think the plants were drawing their nourishment from the women, he thought.

All the same there was something about Martha that touched him. She was a rare organism; he could see that. She probably just needed fertilizer and care to thrive. And maybe that's what he wasn't able to do, the dune inspector, get his women to thrive. He poured all his care and attention into the trees and flowers but forgot the women. Clearly, Thorkild thought, he did not have a sense for women, this brusque man from western Jutland. Thorkild, on the other hand, did, and he was sure he could get Martha to flourish. He had no doubt about that.

So it wasn't many months later when he asked the dune inspector for her hand. The old man's eyebrows shot up on his forehead and he grunted a couple of times as if he had rarely been so surprised, whereupon he gave his consent with a nod.

"I suppose it wouldn't be proper for me to say that you have peculiar taste in women," he said.

꙳ Leo was sitting in the Jeep with Sayeed. Sayeed wasn't moving, he sat there staring straight ahead, but Leo was nervous. The Jeep wouldn't start, and he swore as he tried again and again. But it didn't do any good. So he flung the door open and practically ran out of the car.

"Clemens! God damn it!" he yelled.

Clemens came out of the tent.

"Yes?" he said.

"The goddamn thing won't start!"

"Calm down, Leo," Clemens said.

Leo was about to lay into him, but thought better of it and started kicking the sand instead. A reddish-yellow cloud of dust rose around his boots.

"Piss," he mumbled.

"Just grab the tools," Clemens said, opening the hood.

He leaned in over the engine and checked if maybe the carburetor was plugged or if maybe the wire to the distributor had snapped. But it turned out that the diaphragm in the fuel pump had worn out.

"It's the diaphragm," he told Leo, who was standing behind him with the toolbox.

"Can you fix it?" Leo asked, positioning himself next to Clemens.

"Yeah, if we have a new one," Clemens said. "Go ahead and set that down."

He nodded in the direction of the toolbox. Leo set it down in the sand, and Clemens sat down and started rummaging through it for a new diaphragm.

"Lucky thing we have a mechanic on the expedition," Leo said in a much friendlier tone of voice.

Clemens didn't respond.

"When did you become a mechanic?" Leo asked.

"When? In forty-four. Here we go," he said, standing back up with a new diaphragm in his hand.

"I thought you were just a geologist."

"First I was a mechanic," Clemens said.

"But why?" Leo asked.

"Why?"

"Yeah, why? I mean, you don't look like a mechanic."

"What does one look like?"

Leo smiled.

"Like me," he said.

Clemens straightened up and looked at him.

"Like you?" he asked.

Leo nodded, flung his arms out and looked down at himself.

"Well, all the same, I *am* a mechanic," Clemens said, bending over the fuel pump. "I dropped out of high school after eleventh grade and apprenticed at a garage. And that was that."

"And that was that?" Leo asked.

"You seem very interested."

"I'm trying to get to know you a little!"

"There was a woman," Clemens said.

"Ah, so there *was* a woman!"

"Yes," Clemens said, smiling. "There was a very beautiful woman."

Leo smiled back at him. They didn't say anything. Just smiled. Then Leo asked, "How was she beautiful?"

Clemens took a deep breath and squeezed his eyes shut.

"She had these amazing breasts," he began.

Leo started to smile.

"Well, you're not half as fucking boring as I'd first thought!"

Clemens smiled at him.

"She was a grown-up woman, and I was only seventeen. She was thirty-three."

"No way, man!" Leo said.

"I was in love with her. I was totally obsessed with her, and she'd chosen me out of all the others."

Leo furrowed his brow.

"Imagine going from a thirty-three-year-old woman to seventeen-year-old girls."

He sighed. Leo nodded.

"Yes!" he said.

Clemens wiped the oil off his hands and closed the hood.

"But why did it end?" Leo asked.

His eyes seemed different than Clemens had seen them before. They seemed more accepting.

"He doesn't want to talk about that!" said Anna, who had come over to them without their having noticed. Clemens reached his hand out to her.

"I've often wondered that myself," she said, looking down at the sand. "But it's impossible to get a word out of him."

"You're the one I love now," Clemens said, his eyes suddenly uncertain. He'd completely forgotten about Leo.

"You have a beautiful wife," Leo said. "A very beautiful wife!"

Anna smiled, heat suffusing her.

"Sayeed!" Leo yelled suddenly.

They'd forgotten about Sayeed who was still sitting in the Jeep. Motionless like a pillar of salt.

Clemens shook his head and started packing up the toolbox while Leo went over and pulled Sayeed out of the car.

"How long can you sit without moving?" he asked. "And without saying anything?"

"Longer than you at any rate, Leo," Clemens said, shoving the toolbox into the Jeep again.

≈ Clemens bounded up the stairs. The windows in the stairwell were covered with ice. He squatted in front of one of them and let his finger trace the patterns. A myriad of shapes and figures. As varied as seifs and star dunes in vast deserts. He brought his face closer to the pane so it was almost touching the crystals of ice. Then suddenly he stood and went up the last few steps to Ane.

Clemens pushed open the door. He called out, but his voice was drowned out by Louis Armstrong. She was playing it loud today. Didn't care about the neighbours. He called out again and glanced out into the kitchen. Water was trickling from the faucet into a bowl of dried up yogurt. He turned it off. The living room was empty. Composition books were stacked on the table. The clear, icy light from the window flooded over the stacks. He flipped through them and found his own.

The he pushed open the door to her bedroom. This was where the Louis Armstrong was coming from. She'd moved the record player in here. It was spinning around. The record. He could see it. Way too fast. If the needle weren't holding it in place, it would've flown off and shot through the room like a discus. But now it lay there. Under the needle. Just as Ane lay there, under Thorkild.

From under the enormous shoulders she turned her face to look at him. Her eyes were made of glass. Set in a face of feldspar and silicon.

Clemens backed up. With Ane's scent in his nostrils. And Thorkild's.

50

Copied from Clemens's piece of paper (it was on the verge of disintegrating).

"To Anna Blossom

O you, beloved of my 27 senses, I love your!
You and you, you of yours, you to you, I to you, you to me – us?
Maybe that's out of place!
Who are you, uncounted broad, you are, are you?
People say you'd be.
Let them say it, they don't know how the steeple's standing.
You're wearing your hat on your feet, wandering on your hands,
on your hands you wander.
Hello, your red clothes, sawed into white folds,
Red I love Anna Blossom, red I love your.
You and you, you of yours, you to you, I to you, you to me – us?
Maybe throw that into the cold embers!
Anna Blossom, red Anna Blossom, what do people say?
Bonus Question:
1. Anna Blossom has a bird,
2. Anna Blossom is red.
3. What colour is the bird?
Blue is the colour of your yellow hair,
Red is the colour of your green bird.
You simple girl in your everyday dress,
You sweet, green beast, I love your!
You and you, you of yours, you to you, I to you, you to me – us?

Maybe toss that onto the – fire grate.
Anna Blossom, Anna, A – N – N – A!
I drizzle your name.
Your name drips like tallow.
Do you, Anna, you do know,
People can read you even from behind.
And you, the most splendid of all,
You are from behind as from in front: A – N – N – A.
CARESSING drizzles tallow over my back.
Anna Blossom, you drippy beast,
I – love – your!

AC, May 27, 1958

NORTHEAST OF THE GILF EL-KEBÎR, MAY 1958

❧ After they'd been in camp for a month, the days started to become as unvarying as the desert around them. Sayeed was the first one up. He lit the camp stove and made coffee, although he had been protesting for a long time, trying to get them to drink tea instead. Then the others got up. The men shaved. At least in the beginning. As time passed, that got rarer and rarer, and eventually it was only if someone were going to fetch new supplies in the form of water, gas or food, that they would start doing that kind of thing. And just as the men gave up on shaving, Anna gave up on her hair. She couldn't do anything with it anymore, so either it hung stiffly out over her shoulders or she would wind it up into a bun at the nape of her neck. Not that that made her look civilized – the bun was big and bristly and the hair lay on her head in matted bands.

After breakfast, which they ate under the large awning in front of Anna and Clemens's tent, Leo, Peter, and Clemens would head out to collect samples or look for fossils. Every now and then they'd go together, but usually they each headed off in their own direction, each working his way through his own area. When the heat became unbearable in the middle of the day they would gather again for a few hours in camp. Here they would eat Sayeed's food before cataloguing their findings and various samples. The camp was quiet during these hours. Everyone sat at the folding tables and worked. Anna too.

"What are you writing?" Clemens asked on his way into the tent to get a map.

He stopped, standing just behind her back. She reached out for him and he rested his hand under her chin and raised it so he was looking down into her face. Then she smiled.

"Now why do faces look so crazy when you look at them upside down?"

He smiled, studying her eyes and nose and mouth.

"For the longest time you imagine that it looks totally normal, the face," she said. "But then suddenly you can see that it's completely distorted."

He nodded. She moved his hand.

"To think that we can look like strangers to each other so easily," she said.

"You never answered my question," he said.

"What did you ask?"

"What you're writing."

She shrugged.

"Notes, like the rest of you," she said. "All sorts of things."

He nodded.

"It's good that you have something to do," he said. "Otherwise people just don't make it out here."

"No," she said.

↷ There's a bar down here, mostly it's Arab men inside, but every now and then there's an American or European traveller. They list backward, sliding their backpacks off, then they plop themselves down and cross their legs and swing their feet casually back and forth in those sensible walking sandals they're always wearing, and then they start writing, these travellers, postcards and letters and journals, one page after another, with unparalleled energy and resolve.

But last Friday there was one person who wasn't writing. She just sat there staring out into space, straight ahead, and she wasn't wearing walking sandals, quite the contrary, she was wearing red sandals with narrow leather straps and heels, not some crazy high heel, but still way too high to be practical and sensible out here, I could also see that one strap had been chafing on her heel, and she was always cautiously pushing the strap all the way down on her heel so it wouldn't rub against the sore.

Then she got up and left. And I wasn't ready for that at all.

ᔂ "You're not eating very much, my boy."

It was Clemens's mother. She was standing behind him running her hand through his hair. There were rolls and tea sitting in front of him.

He had become a stranger to her. He'd always been quiet with a tendency to be a bit of an outsider. But all the same he had seemed happy and robust. But now he wasn't eating well or paying attention to his schoolwork anymore. And he was a boy who'd always done his homework. All right, true, it was often with his left hand and while he was doing something else, but still he'd always been the best in his class. But things hadn't gone well on the last test and he'd gotten a bad grade.

But then of course it was a difficult time; she knew that. The time when you become an adult and put your childhood years behind you. Maybe there was something with a girl? She sighed and walked over to the window. From there she could see down over Lake Nørre and over to the cathedral. Lord only knows if Thorkild ever got around to talking to Clemens about all that stuff. About girls. For crying out loud, he was eighteen now. She turned around and looked at him. His back was broad under his sweater, she could see that easily, but when it came right down to it, he was nothing more than a big boy, her Clemens.

She went over to him and put her hands on his head.

"Mom!" he shouted, squirming away.

She pulled her hands back.

"Mom," he said again.

This time his voice had strangled quality to it, as if he were trying to reach out to her and push her away at the same time.

The mood was tense at the dinner table. Martha was nervous. She chatted with the agricultural adviser, who ate dinner with them every Wednesday now that his wife had left him for the organist at the cathedral; at the same time she tried to placate Thorkild, who seemed grumpy and withdrawn. And with all that going on, she was also trying to keep an eye on Clemens. His body was hunched over his soup bowl, and you couldn't see anything other than the top of his head, his shoulders and the hand that was holding the spoon. But at least he was eating. More than he had in a long time.

Actually he was eating an astonishing amount. When he'd drained all the soup from his bowl, he reached for the tureen and ladled another helping into his bowl. Thorkild noticed it out of the corner of his eye but then turned back to the agricultural adviser again who was talking about a mechanical beet harvester that was being developed. It would replace the beet hoe and really would make the farmer's work quite a bit easier. There was no doubt about it. You would pull it behind your tractor, for those who had tractors of course, and by using this kind of attached fork it would then pull the beets up out of the soil, and they would move up a belt that would shake the dirt off them. Marvelous!

Clemens's bowl was almost empty again, and he was tipping it up so he could get the last little bit of soup out. The skin around Thorkild's left eye was twitching. Martha saw it and put her hand on Clemens's arm to get him to knock it off. She smiled apologetically to the agricultural adviser, but luckily he didn't seem to have noticed anything. He was explaining how he didn't think it would be long before it was commonplace to have a tractor, once the war was over, and then this mechanical beet harvester truly would be a real possibility. Clemens pulled his arm away, reached for the tureen again and ladled yet another helping of soup into his bowl.

Thorkild's body tensed as if he were going to stand up. But instead he cleared his throat.

"Clemens," he said.

Martha smiled to the agricultural adviser, and Clemens started eating.

"Clemens!" Thorkild said again.

Clemens set down his spoon, leaned back in his chair and folded his arms. The agricultural adviser stopped talking and stared at him in surprise.

"Clemens, sweetheart," Martha said. "Just leave a little soup for the adviser, OK?"

Clemens ignored her. He was staring at Thorkild. The skin around Thorkild's left eye was twitching again. And now the whole eyelid was quivering along with it.

"Mind your manners," he said urgently under his breath.

Clemens stood up.

"Sit down!" Thorkild said.

A look of doubt flashed across Clemens's face, but then he grabbed the edge of the table, and in an rapid motion he tipped the table over onto Thorkild so the bowls and glasses and piping hot soup crashed down into his father's lap as well as the agricultural adviser's.

"What the hell?" Thorkild yelled, taking a swipe at Clemens.

The agricultural adviser was clutching his napkin and starting to slosh around with it in a puddle of soup. Martha started crying. Now they were beyond her reach. There was nothing more she could do here, and she drew back as Thorkild kicked his overturned chair and stormed over to Clemens who was still standing in the same spot. As his father came closer and closer, he drew himself up. Finally they stood facing each other. Clemens a hint taller, but Thorkild still a bit broader.

"Just who the hell do you think you are?" Thorkild yelled so forcefully that small globs of spit landed on Clemens's face.

Clemens closed his eyes. Either to get rid of a drop of spit on his eyelashes or to take a moment for himself so he could gather the strength it required to remain standing. Every muscle in his body was tensed.

Martha was still crying, and when she saw Thorkild's hand come up to slap the side of Clemens's face, she closed her eyes too. But Clemens managed to deflect the blow and instead planted his fist right in the middle of Thorkild's face. Thorkild doubled over and clutched his nose only to pull his hand away again quickly so he could check and see if there was blood on it. There was. A shiny thread ran from his right nostril to his lip, and redness was spreading out from his nose across his cheek.

Martha screamed and ran over to him. The agricultural adviser stood his chair back up and sat down on it. And Clemens lowered his arm.

A warmth, like after an orgasm, spread through his body, and he left the room.

NORTHEAST OF THE GILF EL-KEBÎR, JUNE 1958

The first signs of heat stroke are headache, dizziness, palpitations, and sometimes profuse sweating. But then the sweating suddenly stops and the skin becomes hot and dry, and the person collapses as if they've suffered a stroke, lying unconscious with contracted pupils and a puffy, bluish-grey face. This is followed by spasms or convulsions, and the body temperature rises to 40–41°C; in some cases getting all the way up to 43–44°C or more. Then death soon follows after increasing limpness and laboured breathing.

In milder cases, consciousness gradually returns, and the patient may recover from the after-effects in about a week's time.

The sharp spike in body temperature is the result of inadequate temperature regulation, which occurs when the body creates a normal or extra amount of body heat, but is unable to radiate enough of the heat because of the elevated temperature of the surrounding air and the cessation of perspiration.

AC, June 10, 1958

59

VIBORG, FEBRUARY 1944

≅ Now Clemens was sleeping with Esther.

Her breasts were small, each with its own hard, little ball inside it. "Ow!" she would say when he touched them.

Clemens's hands slid down over her: shoulders, breasts, stomach, hips. But nothing filled them.

He rolled over onto his back and hid his eyes behind his hands.

"Clemens?" she said.

∾ Now it was Hjørdis.

She was fatter. But without any heft. Everything was perky. Her breasts. Her belly.

As he walked home he remembered the feel of Ane's breasts in his hands. How she would lie on her back and they would slide softly off to the side. How he would gently push them in to feel how they would follow his hands back out again.

And the scent. That dusky scent that emanated from her skin and that got stronger when they made love. It dwelled in her armpits, swam in the beads of sweat across the small of her back, and flowed with the fluids from the mouth of her vagina to settle in a slippery film around her labia and on the insides of her thighs.

NORTHEAST OF THE GILF EL-KEBÎR, JUNE 1958

The Libyan Desert is a vast, arid, rocky plain. The southern portion consists of Nubian sandstone, the northern of nummulitic limestone, while the western portion is pure sandy desert.

The desert plateaus are furrowed with dry valleys, known as wadis, which form whole networks of principal and tributary valleys, very much like river systems and generally exhibiting the same properties. They are presumed to have originated from the rivers that fed the Nile in the Pleistocene.

But occasionally there is evidence of peculiar conditions. In many places the gradient is reversed, and the various valleys intersect like vast labyrinths. This phenomenon, however, is secondary in origin. It is presumably due to the combined effects of very rare downpours, which can wreak havoc on a desert, dry exfoliation, and eolian processes where the winds carry away all the fine particulate matter. These forces are most erosive in places where the strata have already been disrupted by dislocation.

Occasionally, the valleys have been erased and turned into vast basins, and as the original wadis grow wider and wider, an entire desert plateau can be broken down into isolated buttes that grow smaller and smaller through the ongoing dry exfoliation and the work of the winds until, perhaps, they vanish altogether. If the winds expose strata consisting of hard components that do not disintegrate, these will gather on the earth's surface, which will thus be left strewn with fossils and flint concretions. Like bone fragments from enormous, prehistoric creatures.

The lightweight components that stay suspended in the wind for longer are deposited elsewhere as dunes and as sand hills that, with their light colours, contrast with the darker rock walls of the sedimentary mountains.

CC, latitude 24° north, longitude 27° east. June 19, 1958

᪣ They received their signal on the radio. "Say hello to Agnete." Clemens jumped up from his seat in front of the radio and tried to adjust the tuner so there would be less static.

And the next afternoon he felt dizzy as he biked along the tree-lined avenue down to Viborg. It was his first drop, and he was going to be with Jens and Erling. It was raining and the wind gusts, which had picked up over the course of the day, drove the water against him in concentrated sheets. His wet forehead was freezing, but beneath his coat and sweater the revolver was blazing against his skin, and when he noticed the sound of a car somewhere in the darkness, he felt his sphincter suddenly loosen. He was going to lose it, and he strained against it for all he was worth. But that car never did catch up to him. It must have turned onto the road that ran along Lake Nørre.

Clemens took a deep breath, feeling ashamed. He was a fucking man now. A resistance man. He was part of a group. He rode his bike with a revolver tucked in against his stomach. Like a cowboy. On his way to his first drop.

He met Jens and Erling at the old city gate and they rode out of town together on Koldingvej along the train tracks, then past the Viborg Moorland Plantation and the woods at Hald Ege, all the way out to the old Hald Manor House, where they turned southwest until they finally reached the open countryside at Stang Heath. This is where the drop was supposed to take place. Clemens figured they would meet some of the other group members, but there was no one here.

The wind had picked up and it was hurling curtains of rain out over the heath, and the sandy soil at the bottom of the wheel rut they were struggling to push their bikes through was squelching. They'd been drenched for hours, and now that they weren't riding anymore, they quickly got cold. Erling started swearing and kicking his bike when it got stuck in the sandy muck. Clemens reached his hand in to the revolver under his sweater. It felt big and heavy as he eased it up out of the waistband of his pants feeling its weight in his hand, in there under his clothes. He was careful not to let the others see what he was doing. And he was annoyed at the rain and the wind. He'd imagined the first drop completely differently: a warm day in early summer just after sunset. In his mind the sun had always tinted the sky orange and pink, and his hair would take on a bit of that hue as he stood there, his legs apart, holding out lanterns to mark the drop zone. The pilot would show up. First as a faint hum, then as a deep rumble, and finally it would appear on the horizon like a black bird. The Royal Air Force. He would raise the lights to the sky, and afterwards he would salute that pilot up there with the RAF markings on his jacket.

Two bikes materialized out of the drizzle further out over the heath, and Clemens squinted in the rain.

"That's Ditlev and the Butcher," Jens shouted through the wind.

Clemens had heard of the Butcher. People called him that because he worked in a slaughterhouse down on Toldbodgade. Right by Erling's garage.

The Butcher's jaw was broad and meaty. Clemens imagined him sinking his teeth firmly into the cows' flanks as they hung on the meat hooks in the slaughterhouse, and pulling until the flesh loosened and he could rip it off the bones and swallow it.

The Butcher and Ditlev nodded and yelled hello, and Ditlev pointed out over the heath to a place where a clump of juniper bushes stood like tombstones in the wind.

"It's there," he said.

They laid down their bikes in the wheel rut and walked across the heath toward the site. Ditlev tossed the satchel with the flashlights behind one of the bushes, and Erling tried to roll a cigarette, but the paper got too wet too fast.

"Oh well, they taste like shit anyway," he said, tossing the soaked cigarette paper aside.

"When's the pilot supposed to come?" Clemens asked.

He had a sinking feeling in his stomach. He couldn't decide if he was scared or excited.

Jens shrugged.

"He may be here in five minutes, or, it might take two hours," he said.

Clemens nodded, slapping his arms to keep warm. The ice-cold raindrops dripped from his hair down over his face, and there was no point in trying to dry his face because his hands were just as wet.

After another twenty minutes had passed, Ditlev suddenly spun around.

"Listen!" he said.

Everyone concentrated tensely.

"Can you hear that?" he whispered. "It's the plane!"

And now they could hear it, a quiet hum over the rain. They still couldn't make anything out visually, no matter how hard they squinted. The plane got closer and closer and then suddenly Clemens could see it. It broke through the cloud cover and flew toward Ditlev, who was swinging the lanterns. In a moment the containers would slide out of its belly. But then suddenly it started climbing again. Without dropping anything.

The rain was beating against Clemens's face making it hard for him to see the shapes that were pouring out of the underbrush to their right. He staggered backward and stumbled, but got up again. His hands were smeared with mud. And now they were really close, the dogs that the men had with them. They lunged forward until they couldn't come any further because the men were still holding their chains. Then they reared up on their hind legs, froth foaming out of their mouths.

The air was full of shouting and shooting and barking and snarling and bodies moving way too fast. Much faster than Clemens ever imagined they could. He grasped his revolver and started shooting without actually knowing what he was shooting at. Other people were shooting too. Feverishly and frantically. And then he heard a scream. He'd never heard such an awful sound before. He leaped back and scrambled away through the sludgy sand between the heather plants. He felt terrible, on the verge of shitting and wetting himself at the same time.

He flung himself down into an old wheel rut, but a second later a German shepherd was on top of him. A frenzied dog with its slobbering jaws right over his head. He tried to protect his face with his arm, and the dog bit down. His skin burned and pulled, and Clemens felt blood running warmly down his chilly arm. He worked his arm back and forth, but the animal hung on. Then he pulled one leg up under him and with all the strength he could muster he kicked the dog in the balls so it gave a start and a single howl after which it retreated, wheezing and limping.

It was dark now, and Clemens managed to crawl forward on his stomach, further and further away. He had no idea what had happened to the others. If they were dead or had managed to get away. Or, worst of all, if they had been captured.

After a while he found the courage to stand up. The darkness was impenetrable, and there was no way they'd be able to see him. So he ran. With his good hand tight around his wounded forearm. He ran and ran, and he had no other thought but run. "I'm just going to run," he muttered. Run, run. As far away as possible. And he had no idea how long he'd been running, or how far he had come. It was as if his body could never tire. It was no longer a living organism with a finite pool of energy, but an unstoppable machine.

He ran like that until the night was at its blackest. He might have been running for an hour or two or even three. There was no way to know. But suddenly he felt tired. His legs were heavy beneath him, and his arm was hurting more and more. He crawled into an oak-scrub and rested his back against a low, stunted trunk. His heart was beating wildly in his body. "No, no, no," he mumbled in a voice that almost cried out the words as he pulled aside the tattered bits of material from the sleeve of his coat to look at the wound. It looked bad. It wasn't just a row of teeth marks; the flesh was all torn up. He fished his handkerchief out and managed to wind it tightly around the wound using his other hand and his teeth.

"Shit," he said. "Where the fuck is everyone? Stupid shitheads! God damn it!"

And suddenly he was up on his feet again. He hadn't even noticed himself stand up. It must have happened while he was swearing. And then he started running again, but his body was chilled to the bone now and his muscles were stiff and his lungs hurt when he inhaled the cold, wet air. So he wasn't moving very fast anymore. He was just plodding along.

But after a while, he had no idea how long, he spotted a barn. A miserable, tarred-wood building with a sod roof. On the side of the building was a door, which was hanging crookedly on its hinges and which creaked so loudly when he opened it that he feared someone would turn on a light in the farmhouse. He stood for a bit and waited but nothing happened so he tiptoed into the barn. Just inside the door he bumped into a reaper-binder, which he was forced to climb over. Obviously this wasn't the door they normally used. Further in was a cart and loads of harnesses hanging up and also a plough. In the far corner was a pile of straw that reached almost up to the rafters, and he buried himself within it, trying to find a little warmth. The air was thick with dust as he fumbled with the straw and he sneezed a few times. Eventually he started to warm up. And then he fell asleep. Without any transition. Suddenly he was just sound asleep.

He didn't wake up until the sunlight was quivering in small patches on the floor. It was coming in through the cracks in the roof. He lay there for a bit listening, but there was nothing to hear apart from a cow mooing up in the cowshed.

There were informants all over the place by now, and even though he was lying in the straw on a farm in central Jutland he could never be sure. So his heart started galloping again when he heard footsteps in the gravel in the farmyard. He dug himself further down into the straw and tried to breathe as quietly as possible. The footsteps were coming closer and closer and now they were inside the barn. Now it wasn't the sound of gravel he heard anymore, it was the warm sound of feet against the plank floor. And then they stopped. For a while there was nothing to hear, and Clemens rose up a bit so he could peek out. It was a child. A girl. She was standing in the patches of light on the barn floor. She stretched one arm out, looking at the dappled light scattered over her whole body. Then she lifted her face and gazed at the roof.

She jumped. She had discovered Clemens and spun around to run out of the barn, but then she changed her mind and just stood there. Slowly she turned back around so she was facing him. He was still far away, way over in the far corner of the barn. And it wasn't everyday there was a head sticking out of the straw.

"English?" she asked.

"Danish," he answered.

She looked disappointed.

"Are you dying?" she asked then, moving a little closer.

"I don't think so," he said.

She bobbed her chin as if it didn't make much difference.

"You're not peeing in the straw, are you?" she asked.

"Wouldn't dream of it. Is your mother or father home?"

"My father is," she said. "My mother took some eggs over to Kirsten. She usually comes here to buy them, Kirsten does, but we needed some pickled beets and…"

Suddenly she stopped short, blushing.

Then she repeated, "My father's home. Should I go get him?"

Clemens didn't know what to say. On the one hand her father might be a German sympathizer and turn him in right away, on the other hand he couldn't just sneak his way through the entire country for fear of informers. After all there were way more people on his side, and he was going to have to do something about his arm. And besides, he was thirsty. Insanely thirsty, he realized, now that he thought about it.

He nodded.

"Yes, please do," he said, starting to dig his way out of the straw.

She darted off, and he could hear her scurrying over the gravel out there, while she yelled for her father. Clemens climbed out of the straw and walked out into the middle of the barn floor trying to make himself presentable. He brushed the straw off and straightened out his clothes a little, but there really wasn't that much he could do. He looked dangerous. Caked with dried mud and his hair bristling with straw.

It didn't take long before he heard the girl's footsteps scurrying back again. This time followed by heavy, solid steps, and the next instant she was

standing there in doorway to the barn, pointing at him. Her father was a
stocky man with a broad forehead and a weather-beaten face. To Clemens the
man's hands seemed as big as shovels. They stood there for a minute staring at
each other, those two, Clemens and the farmer, as if they were each carefully
considering whether or not they should be afraid of the other. But then the
farmer walked up to Clemens.

"She says you're Danish," he said.

"Yes, I am," Clemens said. "I'm from Viborg."

The farmer nodded, satisfied with Clemens's accent. Then he asked,
"What happened to your arm?"

Clemens held it out.

"I have an injury," he said. "I was bitten by a dog, and it probably needs to
be rinsed out."

The farmer nodded again. He looked like he had a couple of questions
he'd like to ask, but decided it was best not to.

"Well, come on," he said, heading across the farmyard up toward the
house.

The girl skipped along beside him.

"My wife isn't home," he said over his shoulder, "so we'll have to make do
on our own."

The girl tugged on his jacket.

"I *already* told him that," she said looking up at him reproachfully.

They cleaned out the wound, and the man's wife poured a good-sized slosh
of iodine over it when she came home. Clemens ate some food and had some
milk that was creamy and sickeningly sweet because it had come straight
from the cow in the cowshed, and they got him cleaned up a bit.

The farmer felt it was too dangerous for him to go back to Viborg, but
Clemens had to go to find out what had happened to the others. Otherwise it
would haunt him. So he borrowed some of the man's clothes and put on a cap
so he looked like a regular old farmhand, and then they set off in the farmer's
old Ford stakebed truck, which had an open flatbed in the rear and a wood
gas generator on the side.

They reached Viborg without any trouble and Clemens hurried over to
the apartment on Vestergade. They were supposed to meet here if anything
happened. Clemens had memorized the address, but he had never in his
wildest dreams imagined that he would need to use it. The small glimmer
of hope that it held for him was the only thing on his mind, because then
something would happen, then all this would be real. Then he could find a
way to be useful. But now he felt nothing other than the pain in his arm and
the anxiety about what had happened to the others, and what would happen

to him. Because surely he couldn't just go home? It could well be that the Germans were already there waiting for him.

Jens and Erling were up in the apartment. They were pacing around restlessly snapping at each other, and their faces looked grey and drained. Ditlev was dead, shot through the head, and nobody had seen the Butcher. Maybe the Germans had him.

"So that's it – they neutralized our group," Erling said. "They got the Hvidsten group a week ago, we just found that out, and they were probably the ones who…"

"Yeah, yeah," Jens interrupted. "What the fuck would you do if you were hanging by your wrists and they were pressing lit cigarettes into your balls? Huh, Erling? I bet even you'd end up talking some, wouldn't you?"

Erling looked down.

"There's not a fucking man out there who knows how big a hero he is until he's hanging there in that position," Jens mumbled.

"And what about Ditlev?" Clemens asked.

That must've been his scream he'd heard out there. Never had he imagined that a human being could make such a noise.

Jens had been to see Ditlev's wife, and she'd just stood there in the doorway with the little one on her hip and then she collapsed. She didn't make a sound, she just collapsed, and then of course the little one started crying, and Jens just stood there. What could he do? Other than pick the little one up and hold him for a while.

Clemens, who'd been sitting on a chair in the corner this whole time while the other two paced around restlessly, leaned over forward and hid his face in his hands. He wasn't crying. His eyes were dry and irritated. It was the nausea swelling within him. The nausea that had been sloshing around in him for the last twenty-four hours. The nausea that made him close his eyes and prevented him from being able to tell what was going on around him. Not that he couldn't recognize the people and the streets, but everything seemed distorted – as if everything were deformed.

They had to get out of Viborg, and they had to leave immediately. They couldn't wait for the Butcher any longer. He might never show up. He may already be on a train heading south.

They decided Clemens would leave Viborg that day, later in the afternoon. A farmer from down by Lake Tange would be waiting for him at the market square and would drive him to Sahl Heath. But before then there was something he had to do.

Ane jumped when she opened the door to him.

"Clemens!" she exclaimed.

And she made a face he'd never seen her make before. He didn't know this face.

She didn't step aside to let him in, but he started moving in toward her so she was forced to step back and let him past. He went into the living room where he stood with his back to her. She closed the door behind him and stood there just inside the doorway. As if she were in someone else's house. Where she wasn't welcome. She noticed that one of his fists was clenched.

"Clemens," she repeated. So quietly that he almost couldn't hear it. "What's happened?"

Then he turned around.

"What's happened? You're asking *me*?"

He was shouting and the veins and tendons in his neck were writhing like snakes just beneath his skin.

She seemed crestfallen and said, "*Now*, I mean. You look… you look as if…"

He came toward her and involuntarily she took a step back. That made him stop and tilt his head, puzzled, continuing to watch her.

"Are you afraid of me?" he asked.

She looked down and shook her head.

"You are so," he said.

And his face bore an expression she'd never seen before, either. As if he'd discovered a new power.

"What do you want?" she asked.

This time she was looking right at him.

He walked all the way up to her so that she ended up backed up against the door. Then he took hold of her face and kissed her. She tried to turn her face away, but he held it tightly. He was pressing on her jawbone and temples, holding her cranium so hard between his hands that his fingertips turned white around the nails.

Ane was crying. She didn't scream and she didn't yell. She just cried, very quietly, while he pulled her dress up and held her so her back slammed into the door behind her. Then suddenly he stopped. The whole thing only lasted a second. And now he clung to her with his face buried in her neck. And then Clemens was crying. Not silently like Ane, but intensely and convulsively. Until he thrust her aside, tore the door open and ran down the stairs.

~ Anna was sitting in the shade under the awning from the tent, pitting dates. Clemens was sitting at a table on the other side of their campsite with his back to her, studying some maps, and Leo was sitting in the sand a few metres off to the left of her, mending a torn backpack. He was whistling. Sinatra, as always. "I've Got You Under My Skin." Anna grasped one date after the next, and with a steady hand she made an incision down through its wrinkled skin. Now he was humming, Leo. His eyes on the faded backpack. Anna's shirt clung to her back, and she straightened up and peeled it loose from her skin before she huddled back over the dates in the tin bowl again. Now he was singing: "I've got you under my skin, I've got you deep in the heart of me, So deep in my heart that you're really a part of me." He didn't lift his eyes. Clemens turned his head slightly and shot him a quick look before flipping through his maps some more. The wind grabbed at the papers, and Clemens struggled to keep them in place. But soon they were lying flat on the table in front of him again. Anna glanced over at Clemens. "I've got you under my skin, I tried so not to give in, I said to myself, 'This affair never will go so well.'" The sweat streamed down over her face. She looked over there out of the corner of her eye. At Leo. Now he wasn't looking down. He looked her in the eye while carrying on in his calm voice: "But why should I try to resist when, baby, I know so well: I've got you under my skin." Clemens turned toward Leo again and then toward Anna. She put the bowl of dates down and got up and went into the tent behind her. Now Leo just hummed as he pulled the thick needle through the fabric. Clemens pulled his shirt over his head and dried his face with it before tossing it in the sand. He kept working on his maps.

  As time goes by I've come across all sorts of things in mother's book: assorted medical notes, strange scribbling that I have a hard time making heads or tails of, the "Anna Blossom" poem, of course, and then this snippet here that she evidently got from Oskar, her uncle. Boy, did he have all kinds of stuff in his study. I mean, I was there as a kid and it's true – he never cleaned the place, "I know exactly where everything is," he would assure us. The papers were deposited in archeological layers, one on top of the next, and if you wanted to find something all you had to do was dig through the layers. And since Oskar also had an amazing memory, he always knew what came after what in these piles; his brief and sudden interest in angels, for example, came before his work on nominalizations, and one day when for some reason or other he wanted to find his way down to a linguistics article on these nominalizations he caught sight of the book about angels, browsed through it and called my mother over to him – she was probably lying on his ottoman reading – and he showed her the book with its florid sentences that moved down over the page like the weft in a tapestry.

And my mother was moved, as she was by all sorts of things, and thought that that's how it was with angels and heaven. A body. Heaven was a body – and my mother, who's always been so preoccupied with bodies.

From Uncle Oskar's old book about angels, De Natura Angelorum, I. It was written by a Benedictine monk by the name of Venanzio of Perugia (Joseph wouldn't have it).

The angels can be divided into three classes: the Good, the Capricious, and the Wise.

72

It has often been my experience that the angels are fully and completely aware that all heaven is a body. In the most off-handed manner they will discuss such and such a relative who lives in some part of the chest or some part of the lower back.

Like human beings, angels have clothing that they put on or take off and set aside until they need it again. Angels dress according to their type, such that the Wise wear clothes that sparkle like flame, the Capricious wear raiment that glows luminously, while the Good wear light, white clothing that lacks any lustre.

There is an atmosphere that gives sound to the speech of both angels and humans; and like humans, angels inhale this atmosphere, and their words slide out into the world with their exhalation. When the angels address people, they do not speak their own language; rather, they speak the language of the people or another language that the people understand. This is because the angels merge with the person, and by this means both share the same thoughts. When one human speaks to a second, the speech flows first into the air and, via this external pathway, it continues until it reaches the auditory organ of the addressee, through which it makes its way inside. By contrast, the speech of an angel flows first into the person's mind and, via an internal pathway, continues to this person's auditory organ, and hence its movement is from the inside. Therefore anyone who is in the same room, but has not been addressed by the angel, cannot hear its speech. An angel's speech can even flow into the tongue and cause it to vibrate slightly.

Different humans feel related to different angels, some to the Wise, others to the Capricious, and still others to the Good. This is because wise angels share tendencies and thoughts to a greater extent with some people than with others. After having studied this carefully for years and discussed it at length with the angels, I have realized that it can be summarized as follows: the good angels are angels for people who have settled down and for the chaste; the capricious angels are angels for thieves and travellers, for the lost and the lecherous, for the children and the souls of the dead, for the lyre players and the soothsayers, for the fire and the deceitful, for the businessmen and for the dreams; and the wise angels are angels for the rest."

AC, August 11, 1958

෨ I called home to Mette the other day. That was before I found out where they are. I wanted her to go out to their house and see if my mother's doctor's bag was there. And thank God it wasn't there. She must have it with her. That's comforting to me.

Mette had tidied up the house a little, she said. They'd left in a hurry, and had left an awful mess behind. My father's rock collection – of pyrite and pyrrhotite, sphalerite and cairngorm, rose quartz and tigereye, petrified wood and hematite – was scattered all over the floor, and my mother's carpets were strewn around at random. Yes, she'd started weaving, my mother, after that expedition in fifty-eight. She wasn't able to go back to the hospital until January of sixty. She was far too unwell when they got back, so she started weaving.

As I read her notes from the expedition, it actually doesn't surprise me in the least that she poured her heart and soul into her weaving. I have to say.

SAHL HEATH, VIBORG, AND COPENHAGEN, MARCH 1944 TO AUGUST 1949

 Jens and Clemens wound up in the same place. Sahl Heath down by Lake Tange.

It was starting to get dark when the farmer dropped them off by a small, whitewashed tenant farm on the edge of the heath. There was a farmhouse with three windows on each side and a stable attached to the house at a right angle. The walls were cracked and two of the windows in the farmhouse were boarded up with masonite.

The stable was littered with enormous bundles of straw-rope and empty sacks. The posts dividing the stalls and the manure gutters that ran along both sides of the centre aisle were crusted over with dried cow manure. And the whitewash on the walls had yellowed and mildewed from the damp.

"What the hell kind of pigs lived here?" Jens growled in annoyance.

Clemens didn't say anything. It almost seemed like he thought this was the best he could expect.

A wall of stench from mildew and dust hit them as they opened the door from the stall to the house. The table in the living room was fashioned out of a half-rotten, worm-eaten wooden wagon bed mounted on rickety, mismatched legs, each one a different length so the table teetered if you so much as touched it with your hand.

Jens tossed his bag into a corner, put his hands on his hips, and looked around.

"Well, there's certainly a lot to be done here," he said, nodding.

Jens was from way out by Stavsholm just north of Harboøre, so he hadn't seen much of the world. Clemens couldn't remember how many brothers Jens had, but he'd always pictured a crooked little house with skinny boys hanging out of the windows and a door that bulged outward because it could barely contain all the brothers. Jens was the oldest, and someday he would inherit the house and the struggle to get enough to grow in the tiny plot of sandy, impoverished soil that belonged to the tenant farm. There'd never been much land, but now there was almost nothing because for generation after generation they'd had to divide it up among the sons.

And now Jens was standing here in the mouse-infested living room of a ramshackle tenant farm in Sahl Heath proclaiming that there sure was a lot of work to be done.

Clemens couldn't take it.

"You're just grateful for whatever little scraps you get, aren't you, Jens?" he asked from where he was sitting in a tattered armchair.

With an astonished look on his face, Jens turned toward Clemens.

"What do you mean?" he asked.

"You'll just put up with anything, won't you? They could offer you the biggest load of crap and you'll just make the best of it, won't you?"

Clemens looked up at him in derision and disgust and Jens punched the table next to Clemens with his fist and disappeared out into the darkness.

But a little over an hour later he was standing there again. He looked like he'd forgotten the whole thing.

"Look over here!" he yelled from out in the kitchen.

Clemens got up reluctantly.

"I got us some food," Jens said, unfolding brown paper to reveal four thick pieces of mettwurst.

Clemens looked surprised.

"And milk," Jens said, holding up a glass canning jar with a piece of cheesecloth for a lid.

Clemens smiled, shaking his head. He was in a much better mood now. It was amazing that Jens could leave this shack for an hour in the middle of the night and come back with milk and mettwurst.

"Where the hell did you scrounge up sausage from?" Clemens asked, searching for a frying pan.

"Well, finders keepers," Jens muttered, lighting the little camping stove that was standing on the kitchen counter. The blue flame sputtered and whistled until he adjusted it.

They spent the next few days trying to fix up the house a little bit. They dumped most of the ruined furniture into the stable, aired the place out, and swept with the broom they found in the old milking parlour. It looked as if someone had bitten off the middle bristles so they could only sweep with the two remaining tufts, one on each side.

They did a decent job in those few days. They didn't think about much, they concentrated on the cleanup, forced to use what energy they had left struggling with the heavy furniture, even though Clemens's wound hurt. But it seemed to be healing nicely now.

They also spent some time getting to know the area. There was a little grocery store a kilometre and a half from the house. The grocer had been the one who had found the farm for them in the first place. He allowed them to buy things on credit, and he had a telephone they could borrow if they ever needed one. And then there was the farm Jens had visited on that first night to barter for a little milk and food. The people there were nice, too, and Jens and Clemens were able to go over there every evening at milking time and they would fill their jar with milk. And little by little Clemens even got used to the milk's creamy consistency while Jens would take big gulps, drying his milk mustache off with the back of his hand and proclaiming that it was much better than beer.

But once they had fixed the house up some and became accustomed to walking down to the grocery store for sardines and rye bread and fetching milk from the farm, something happened to Clemens.

Whereas Jens remained energetic, coming up with ideas for things that ought to be done and that might make their primitive everyday lives easier, Clemens got quieter and quieter and his eyes narrower and narrower. They took on an "I told you so" expression. Here he was, eighteen years old, wasting the most valuable thing he had. He was wasting his youth, that's how he felt. The few years when his body was bubbling with vitality. Because what was left after twenty-five? Well, really twenty-two? That's when the laziness and indifference would start to set. He knew it. And now he was missing out on these years. Everything had been so promising for him and now it was all gone: he should've been fighting for his country, he should have been making love to his woman, he should have graduated from high school and then gone to Copenhagen for college. And now he was sitting here in a tattered armchair in a house with masonite boards over the windows with some guy named Jens. A scrawny hick from Stavsholm in western Jutland who was perfectly content here because he didn't aspire to anything better, because he wasn't cut out for anything more. But it was different for Clemens. He felt a pressure in his chest as if something or someone was trying to suffocate him. At first he wanted to scream, but as time went on he got used to it and wouldn't do anything besides snap at Jens and stare at him condescendingly as he went about trying to make traps.

As the spring wore on, Clemens sank down deeper and deeper into this state of imagined self-importance and meaninglessness. Jens generally let him be and tried to focus on his own life, which only rarely overlapped with

Clemens's. Once in a while it got to be too much for him, and then he would leave for a couple of days, when he would wander around on the heath or in the plantation, or else he would pound his fist on the table somewhere and yell that for Pete's sake, enough was enough. But when on June 6 they heard from the grocer, who had a radio in the back of his store, that the Allies had landed at Normandy, Clemens's eyes opened a little, and he took the grocer up on his offer of a beer. But it was a long summer, and it took the Allies a lot longer to get to Paris than Clemens had first imagined it would on that spring day in the grocery store. They didn't do that until August 29.

That day Clemens shaved off the beard that had covered his face since March and he succeeded in getting a lift to Viborg. Jens was going to stay in Sahl Heath. It was still way too risky to go back, he figured. But Clemens didn't care. What did he have to lose, he said. He had no girlfriend, he had no high school diploma, and he had no father. And now he couldn't stay here any longer. Not a day longer.

So Clemens had to say goodbye to Jens. To Jens, whom he had despised for being satisfied with so little. But when they stood facing each other in front of the house, the old image started to come back: the image of Jens with the steady hands who had showed him how to attach the time pencils. And he looked at those hands hanging at the tall man's sides. These big but bony hands that were so kind and at the same time could slam into the table with a force that made both the rotten wooden wagon bed and the table legs shake.

Of course there wasn't anything to say. What could Clemens say? The last five months of thoughts and feelings had been like a knot – so tortuous that it seemed impossible to get hold of an end anywhere to try to untangle the thing. The knot was so dense he could not dig his fingers down into it to even start trying to unravel it. Of course, there wasn't anything to say. So Clemens clapped Jens on the upper arm and looked him in the eye. And Jens nodded back. He'd never been one to carry a grudge, the Bone Man from Stavsholm. That was his name, Clemens thought as he turned around to wave to Jens, who was still standing at the same spot outside the house, the Bone Man from Stavsholm.

So it happened that Clemens walked into Erling's old garage in Viborg at the end of August 1944. But of course Erling wasn't there. What was he thinking, the boss asked pulling him into the office. Erling was at a garage in Valby just outside of Copenhagen. The boss had arranged it himself. But he'd give Clemens the address if he promised to be careful with it. So it didn't fall into the wrong hands.

Clemens roamed around the streets of Viborg. His parents' home in Asmildkloster was on the other side of town, but he couldn't go there. And not because of the Germans. So instead, he wandered around aimlessly and didn't stop until he was standing on Ane's street, in the doorway across from her apartment. He couldn't see anything up there, apart from a withered geranium, a stack of books, a sewing chest and the bottom edge of the blackout curtains, which were hanging, rolled up at the top of the windows.

Suddenly he saw Mini come walking around the corner. Ole, arm in arm with Hjørdis, was next to him. She was smiling, gazing up at Ole, while Mini skipped along next to her. All three of them were wearing Danish-style graduation caps.

Clemens ducked back into the doorway. He felt a sinking feeling in his stomach.

He had to go to Valby to see Erling. There was no getting around it. But before that he'd have to get some money and a place to stay before the eight o'clock curfew that night. He'd heard about the curfew, which had been in effect since June 25, but he hadn't paid much attention to it out on the heath.

So, in the end, he was forced to go there. To Asmildkloster.

The very next day he was sitting on the train for Copenhagen. He'd gotten some money and clothing, and his mother had hugged him and cried, looking thin, her face pallid, and his father had tried to reach out to him as he walked away, but had given up and let his arm sink back down. Clemens found it hard to forget the look in his father's eyes. The image was burned onto his retinas, and several times during the ride he got up and went to the bathroom and splashed water on his eyes to cool them.

Clemens reached Erling's garage in Valby that afternoon, and he hugged Erling so hard that the guys booed and whistled and yelled faggot at him, but Clemens didn't hear anything. He felt only the burning in his eyes and a dizziness that he didn't pay much attention to, because he knew that Erling had him now.

And so Clemens finally made it to Copenhagen. But not with a high school diploma and not starting at the university as a freshman the way he had always pictured it. No, he was standing in a garage in the Valby neighbourhood with a mechanic's rag stuffed in his pocket and a smoke hanging out of his mouth.

Clemens stayed at the garage until he was drafted in September 1946. He spent the last four months of his required military service until 1947 in Germany's Friesland district and its capital, Jever, where the Danish soldiers had taken over occupation duties from the British. When he wasn't lying under a truck or didn't have his arms buried up to the elbows in its engine, he was driving supplies around. Everywhere he saw rubble and rocks and hunks of cement piled in mounds like caved-in mountains and women whose eyes were black with fear and hunger carrying around children whose faces already looked like old men's.

The plan was that after his military service he would go back to the garage, but instead of biking out to Valby, he headed straight for the high school equivalency program at the Frederiksberg School of Adult Education, where he was lucky enough to get a spot even though the other students were already a month into the program.

He started suffering from that familiar sinking feeling in the pit of his stomach again. The feeling that he was throwing his life away – a feeling he'd gotten so used to during the war when he was in Sahl Heath. It had started percolating through him again at the end of his time at the garage in Valby and again in Germany during all those supply runs.

Two years later, in June 1949, he graduated. It had been five years since he'd ducked back into the doorway as Mini and Ole and Hjørdis walked by in their graduation caps. He should have been walking with them then, he should have been hopping along next to Mini or walking arm-in-arm with Hjørdis. Where would he be now if he'd graduated on time? And who would he be?

He was almost twenty-four years old and had learned that nothing was permanent or stable in this world, that everything could change faster than he could comprehend. What was joy and desire one day would be pain and hatred the next.

But then he realized that there was a world beyond people, a world that wasn't affected by people's perpetual, unpredictable fickleness, a world that changed only at an infinitesimal pace and that people had only an incredibly limited effect on, that there was something much bigger, there were continental plates with fault lines running between them, there were sedimentation and erosion, there were rocks and mountains that changed shape through nothing more than the action of water and wind, and that all this took place over millennia, that he could sit for days watching waves crash against the rocky shore but still not see any change in the stone; once he realized all this, he enrolled in the Geology Department at the University of Copenhagen.

  Leo and Clemens were sitting around the fire in folding chairs when Anna came out of the tent. Leo's legs were stretched out in front of him and his hands clasped behind his head as he stared up into the high, high desert sky. The sun had long ago pulled its heat and fiery reds down with it, leaving the desert a sparkling blue wasteland. Clemens was leaning over a mug of whiskey he was holding with both hands. He looked up as the faded tent flap flipped aside and Leo lowered his chin a little so his field of vision could just accommodate both the desert sky and Anna. She stepped out and with long, even strides strolled into the flickering sea of light cast by the fire. She was holding her book in her hand.

"They were teeming with sexual desire!" she said. "The angels. You know, I don't think people really get that."

Her hair lay like dark reeds around her face, jutting out over her shoulders. A turban covered her forehead all the way down to her eyebrows and a sweater that was way too big hung down over her thighs all the way to the gash of skin at her knee below the linen pants that weren't quite long enough to reach her leather boots.

Clemens's eyes shone as he stared intently at Anna, who with a touch of surprise was looking at Leo, doubled over in a hearty belly laugh so that his foot was about to tip over the bottle of whiskey that was standing in the sand between him and Clemens. Then she swept her eyes over to Clemens. His eyes were twinkling, his mouth listing to one side of his face, trying to suppress his laughter.

"What's so funny?" she asked.

Leo tumbled off the rickety chair and only just barely managed to grab the bottle before it toppled over.

"The way you look!" he wailed. "And you're talking about sexual desire!"

"Drunken idiots!" she hissed, striding over and grabbing the bottle out of Leo's hand.

Clemens braced his elbows against his knees and rubbed his face with his hands. But Leo leapt up and grabbed hold of Anna's forearm before she was able to pour the whiskey out into the fire. He pushed her back until she bumped into the Jeep and couldn't go any further. With his hand still firmly holding her forearm he leaned his body in over hers.

"You're drunk and pathetic!" she said.

"Leo, let go of her, you're drunk!" Clemens shouted from inside the light, squinting his eyes to make out their shapes out in the darkness.

Anna was almost as tall as Leo and when he pressed his body closer to hers, his hot whiskey breath surrounded her face.

"*You're* teeming with sexual desire," she said.

Leo let go of Anna's arm and spun around on his heels but then stopped suddenly.

Clemens was standing right in front of him.

Leo stood completely motionless, staring Clemens straight in the eye. A glint of a sneer appeared in his eyes.

"If you don't move now," Clemens hissed almost inaudibly, "I'm not going to be able to control myself any more!"

At that moment Anna grabbed hold of Clemens's sleeves and tried to pull him along.

"Clemens," she said. "Come on."

Clemens kept staring at Leo.

"Come on," Anna repeated, holding one of his arms.

Reluctantly, he allowed himself to be pulled along.

"That's the last time, Leo! Otherwise I'm going to have to send you away," he said.

Anna pulled the tent flap aside and pushed Clemens in before her. She zipped it shut behind them and went over to Clemens who had sat down on the cot with his face resting in his hands.

Anna crawled around behind him and ran her fingers through his hair, which was stiff with sand and salt. After a while he let his hands fall and leaned his head back. His eyes were closed. Her hands slid down around his chin and up over his jaw. His stubble prickled against her palms. Her fingers felt their way along, skimming around the edges of his nostrils, up over the sharp bridge of his nose and along his eyebrows, which lay as straight as rulers, glistening with salt below his forehead where the wrinkles were just starting to show in the taut skin.

Anna pulled up his sweater and shirt. He helped her and then tossed his clothes aside. He had a farmer's tan, the back of his neck and his forearms were dark brown, but his back was as white as paper. She licked the transition between the two colours on his neck and with her tongue she felt the small, bristly hairs that grew below his hairline. Then she turned his shoulders and pressed him down on the cot so he was lying on his back, and with her tongue she exposed his almost covered nipples.

Anna was in that place where everything else other than herself and Clemens faded into the background. It was like being in a movie that was playing backward. She could see and smell and feel so clearly that it almost hurt.

HARDANGER PLATEAU, JULY 1950

᷎ Clemens had learned how to do this from Thorkild. With unfailing precision Clemens shaved the blade along the birch logs. The bark coiled up – just like the stalk of a dandelion curls up when you split it – leaving a wound where the bare wood was exposed. Then he peeled off some bits of bark and arranged them under the three logs he'd nestled on top of each other on the little patch of bare, black dirt that remained after he'd raked away the moss and reindeer lichen.

Clemens was in Norway with his friend Gustav. Gustav was also a geology student, and they had spent countless evenings together at each other's apartments in Copenhagen but had never traveled together before. This was also the first time Gustav had ever been to the mountains.

While Clemens was lighting the campfire, Gustav went down to the river to get water. When he got back the fire was blazing and Clemens was bent over the hare he had shot earlier in the day. He skinned the animal and hung it up over the fire on a rack he had fashioned out of branches.

The next day they passed the tree line and made their way in over the mountains toward Finse, the highest point on the Oslo Bergen train line. To their south was the blue ice of the Hardangerjøkulen glacier and to their north the massive Hallingskarvet Ridge, formed millions of years ago when the bedrock was shoved up over the plain.

There were large herds of reindeer over toward Haugastøl. There were cloudberries and crowberries, and there were ptarmigans with rusty yellow stripes and bits of white along the edges of their feathers.

They slept in their canvas tent, peed behind the dwarf birch, and drank from the streams that carried the meltwater from the glaciers past the moss and dwarf willows. They crossed the perennial snow, leaving tracks from their hiking boots on its surface, which ordinarily was icy and hard. And they stopped at cairns built by people who knew the risks of getting lost in the wilderness. But tonight they were going to stay at the Norwegian Trekking Association cabin up in Finse.

The cabin was low to the ground, as if it were hunkering down to get out of the wind. Next to it was a lake of black water without any vegetation around it other than what had managed to creep forward, low and elongated, over the layer of topsoil that tried, like thin skin, to cover the bones of the bedrock.

Like the cabin and the thin layer of moss, Gustav also seemed to be hunkering down, as if the sky and the vast wilderness around him were weighing him down, and when he stepped out of the wind into the cabin he tried to put the mountainous landscape outside out of his mind. Better inside this cabin in the middle of nowhere than outside in that God-forsaken wasteland he'd just closed the door on.

But Clemens flung his backpack down enthusiastically onto one of the bunks in the bedroom, pulled off his boots and then the damp wool socks and lay down on the crimpy wool mattress.

"Ah!" he exclaimed.

Gustav cast a sidelong glance at him from his spot on the opposite bunk, where he carefully removed one sock. The yarn was sticking to the moist sore on his heel that was starting to smell.

Unlike the other cabins, where supplies were brought in by horseback, the cabin at Finse was right on the rail line to Bergen and was therefore kept well stocked with sweet brown cheese and cured mutton and smoked sausages and sour cream porridge.

Gustav and Clemens sat down at the big square table in the dining room. They said hello to the others. Seven men and two women. All Norwegians apart from Halvorsen, who was Swedish.

Halvorsen was actually a pianist by training, but when he'd developed arthritis in his fingers he got himself a compass, locked the door to his apartment in Stockholm, and just set out heading northwest. Two weeks later he crossed the Norwegian border at Lekvattnet. And now Halvorsen was sitting here with his curly beard and parchment skin eating meatballs and sour cream porridge.

When Gustav went to bed, Clemens sat down by Halvorsen, and they started drinking hard. First beer and then moonshine. Halvorsen reported he had seen both bears and wolves in the forests around the Norwegian border and that he had been so scared that he shit his pants and it streamed down his thighs. But the bears and wolves ended up not being a big deal. The little shepherd boy he found near Mårbu last fall had been much worse.

Halvorsen had been caught off guard by the weather in October and he had been smack dab in the middle of the mountains with the cold searing his skin and the snow drifting around him and pushing its way into his nose and mouth. He had to walk with his eyes squeezed shut, just keeping them open a tiny crack. He had long since become disoriented in the snowstorm and darkness when he suddenly stumbled upon one of those rustic structures they call a *seter*, intended for use as a bunkhouse in the summer when the cows were grazing in the high meadows. The door was almost buried in a snowdrift, and it took Halvorsen quite a while to dig it clear and make it inside. Inside he focused all his strength against the door and managed to get it closed again behind him before collapsing on the floor. The cold radiated from the walls, and the temperature was pretty much the same inside as out. But he was out of the wind and driving snow. He could open his eyes all the way and gradually he was able to make out the room he was sitting in.

Halvorsen crawled over to the fireplace and the pile of rags lying in front of it, but when he tugged on one of them, it wouldn't budge. Turned out it was a boy lying there. Wrapped up in those dirty rags.

He had gotten lost. He had come into the mountains with the girls who look after the cows and when it was time to head back down they couldn't find him. They had searched for him and waited to go back until they didn't dare stay up there any longer for fear that the snow and cold would trap them there some morning when they woke up.

The boy had found his own way back to the seter two days after the girls had left it with the sheep, and when Halvorsen found him he was listless and cold in front of the fireplace, which was just as cold as the boy. The girls had left flatbread and corned beef in the seter building, but after seven days there wasn't much left, and the boy had been living off of lichen and whatever he could find in the way of berries and roots. There wasn't any more firewood either, and the boy had broken apart the storage bench and footstools and burned them along with the dried dung from the sheep and reindeer.

His lips were blue, but Halvorsen saw the pulse beneath the skin on his throat. Weak, as though it were coming from far away, but it was there, and Halvorsen lifted the boy up into his arms. He looked around for more blankets or rags, but there was nothing in the building, so he lay down on his back on the floor and tucked the boy under his parka and Icelandic sweater and the thin wool jerseys he wore on the inside, against his skin. The boy's whole upper body and the top of his thighs fit in there. He was so big, Halvorsen was, and the boy just a little tyke of six or seven. With his arms around the boy, Halvorsen eventually fell asleep and when he woke up again, the body against his belly and chest wasn't freezing cold anymore. Halvorsen's heat had penetrated into it, but it was still motionless.

He left the boy lying on the floor for a second while he searched the space again for food and clothing. But the boy had beaten him to it. So he had no choice but to try to get him down from the mountain as fast as possible.

Halvorsen took the clothes off his upper body and dressed the boy in his wool jerseys and the Icelandic sweater. He kept the parka for himself. Then he picked the boy up and carried him down the mountain to the closest settlement, Bjørkeflåta.

It wasn't snowing anymore, and he was able to get his bearings from the sun and stay on course toward the east-northeast. Mostly the boy hung limply against Halvorsen, with his head resting on Halvorsen's shoulder, but every now and then he would whimper, and then Halvorsen would sit down and try to melt a little snow between his hands and let the half-thawed scoop slide into the boy's mouth. Then he would proceed. Twelve hours later he staggered down toward the few farms that constituted Bjørkeflåta.

The scent of birch smoke and sheep hit him, and after he passed a black storage building and was standing in front of a log house with tiny windows, he started to sob.

A woman opened the door, and when she saw what he was carrying in his arms she hustled him into the house, yanked the blankets off the box bed and signalled to Halvorsen that he should set the boy down there. Another woman appeared and together they got the cold clothes off the boy and wrapped him up in a sheepskin and several woven blankets. Meanwhile Halvorsen allowed himself to sink down on the bench inside the door and fall asleep leaning over the table. The women heated milk for the boy and tried to pour it between his lips. Most of it ran out again and flowed down over his chin, but some stayed in, and little by little the boy lost his transparent look.

Halvorsen developed a fever that night. It took three days before he could see straight again and then the boy, whose name was Arnfinn, was sitting there staring at him. Halvorsen held his hand out to the boy, palm up. The boy peered at the hand and Halvorsen nodded. Then Arnfinn laid his hand in Halvorsen's and Halvorsen closed his around the boy's.

Clemens didn't say anything and Halvorsen was also quiet. They were both red in the face, and Clemens's eyes glistened. He kept studying the big man who was sitting there, heavy and immobile, like he had been carved from the bedrock outside. His hands were broad and full of flakes of hard skin.

Halvorsen raised his hands.

"Yup," he said, nodding toward Clemens. "You'd never know that they were once some of the best hands in Sweden."

Clemens gazed into Halvorsen's pale blue eyes.

"They moved much faster than my thoughts. They were like birds over the keys."

He laughed.

"But then they got sluggish and reluctant. They didn't want to do it anymore."

Clemens still didn't say anything. He looked down.

"And so, I sold my baby grand and bought a compass."

He fished a scratched compass up out of his breast pocket and started unwinding the red cord he'd wound around it.

"The craziest damned thing," Halvorsen began as he fumbled with the cord, "is that the music came with me. It's been in my head the whole time."

He put his face in his hands and shook his head.

"The whole time."

Clemens wanted to reach out and hold those hands, pull them away from Halvorsen's face. But obviously he didn't. He had also had way too much to drink, and you should never act on your first impulse when you've been drinking. He knew that. But there was something inside him that he hadn't noticed before. It was almost like being in love, but warmer, as if all his bodily fluids were boiling, on the verge of spilling over the whole time and pouring out his eyes.

Halvorsen rubbed his face with his hands. Then he smiled at Clemens.

"All these longings," he said. "Soon a person's going to be nothing more than a bundle of longings."

"Do you really hear it all the time?"

"What?" Halvorsen asked.

He was pouring more into their glasses.

"Do you really hear the music all the time?"

"Do you like music?" Halvorsen asked.

Clemens shook his head.

"No... yes," he said. "I don't know."

Halvorsen tipped his head back and gulped down the liquor.

"I would really have liked to have heard yours," Clemens said. So quietly that Halvorsen almost couldn't hear him. And immediately after that Clemens turned red. Halvorsen turned toward him, and even though Clemens knew the skin on his face was burning and his eyes were way too intense, he kept looking at Halvorsen. His chest was tight. This warmth was unfamiliar, and he felt both happy and as though he were about to cry because this great man was looking at him like this.

Halvorsen nodded.

"I would've loved to have played for you too," he said.

One of the women came in and put a little wood on the fire before leaving the room again.

"Tell me: what it is *you* long for," Halvorsen said.

Clemens furrowed his brow and sat up in the chair.

"Long for?" he asked.

Was there something he longed for? Other than to be Arnfinn? But of course he couldn't say that.

He looked at Halvorsen helplessly.

"I don't think I long for anything."

"Then tell me why you're here. You're so young. I would've thought you'd be sitting in Copenhagen drinking beer with your school friends."

Clemens took a deep breath.

"It's so quiet here," he said. "It's so quiet in the mountains. So quiet that I can hear my own blood."

Halvorsen nodded.

"I love the mountain plateaus," Clemens continued.

He was warming up to the subject, he noticed. Now he didn't see Halvorsen or the room they were sitting in. Now he saw only the bryophytes and the reindeer moss that stretched out and away and didn't disappear until his eyes couldn't reach that far anymore. When his eyes ran into the water. And he saw the rocks and the cliffs and the mountains, and nothing moved other than a few rocks in a talus slope, and there was nothing to hear besides a ptarmigan and a glacier calving into a lake, and he could inhale air from the sky above him, so freely and deeply that his ribcage would almost burst.

"Up here it's like I can feel how big the world is," he said. "And how little of it we humans take up. We're nothing, and we mean nothing."

Halvorsen wrinkled his brow.

"But you're taking up quite a bit of my field of vision right now," he said.

"Well, sure," Clemens said. "I mean, because we're sitting here. But if I go stand out there, then I'll hardly take up any space." He fidgeted.

"That feeling scares Gustav," Clemens said. "But not me."

"Maybe it's like standing in one of those big cathedrals," Halvorsen said. "Whenever I did that, I always felt like that. Just that sense of space, that it's so vast."

Clemens smiled.

"So, being in the mountains is like being in a church?" he asked.

"I've never been religious," Halvorsen said. "But I've always been dreadfully sentimental. A church is filled with the sighs of grieving people. It always hits me square in the chest. I can see them all there in front of me, centuries' worth of people praying and pleading and mourning."

He smiled ruefully and shook his head.

"So whenever I'm in a church I'm always twisting and turning around, sensing all these people." He fumbled with his glass. "And, damn it, it's not even because I'm getting old. I've always been like this."

"So you see and sense people all over the place?" Clemens said.

Halvorsen smiled again.

"And you see mountains and glaciers?"

Maybe they experienced the people and the mountains in the same way. Maybe that's what it was, Clemens thought. Maybe that was the intense feeling he experienced up here in the mountains but that he wasn't able to share with anyone. Maybe they had this feeling in common, he and Halvorsen.

And the feeling of emptiness.

Because Clemens had realized this evening that he was carrying an emptiness around inside him. That he longed for something. But he wasn't sure what it was. After all, he had his studies, he had these trips to the mountains, he had his women. And he had plenty of those.

"It's like I'm a little – " he began. But stopped short.

"Yes?" Halvorsen prompted, reaching out his hand toward Clemens. With his palm up as if he were waiting for Clemens to give him something.

Clemens looked down at the hand. It contained a whole landscape of ravines and slabs of slate, of footpaths and roads. Worn and traveled.

"I've never talked about this stuff before," Clemens said.

Halvorsen set his hand down on the tabletop, but left it out.

"I always want to cry when I'm alone in the mountains," Clemens admitted, smiling apologetically. "I want to collapse onto the ground, sobbing."

He lowered his face, looking askance at Halvorsen. With a rueful expression. As if he'd just entrusted him with the most painful truth about himself. But Halvorsen didn't laugh. He nodded and looked down at the glass he was fumbling with in his one hand. Then he took a deep breath.

"That feeling you're talking about," he said, "I know it well."

Clemens looked up. Then he started talking, but faster this time.

"I don't know if what I'm feeling is euphoria or terror to be standing there in the middle of all those mountains."

"Perhaps you feel enormous and miniscule at the same time," Halvorsen said. "Miniscule because you're nothing but a grain of sand in the enormity of the whole natural world, and enormous because you're a part of it."

Clemens nodded and started talking, but Halvorsen interrupted him.

"That's how I feel in those big churches. I'm miniscule in the enormous space of the church, and I'm miniscule – just one little person – compared to all the people who've stood or sat in that space over the centuries. And all the stories they've brought in there with them. But I'm big because I have all these people and their stories in me. And because I'm a part of this vast succession of people."

He spoke gesturing wildly with his hands and nearly knocking over the bottle of liquor.

"And when I was composing music, I felt big, I was big while the notes and sequences were coming to me. You have to be big right then. And I was big when I was carrying Arnfinn down from the mountain. I had to be, otherwise I would never have believed I could do it. But afterwards you always have to find your way back to your proper size again."

Clemens sat there for a while without saying anything, but then he started talking again. This time reluctantly.

"But I think there's something else, too," he said. "When I'm out there in the mountains, it's like all the colours and smells and sounds are clearer, almost like they're permeating my body."

He took a deep breath. He felt like he was searching for words he didn't know. And he didn't know where to look for them, or even if he had the words in him at all. Apparently, it was much easier for Halvorsen. But then of course he was also used to hearing noises in his head. Well, music anyway. But I wonder if there isn't a connection there somewhere all the same, Clemens thought.

"Sometimes," he continued, "I almost feel like I'm floating out over the terrain, or flowing into it. I feel like I almost become one with it. And then maybe a second later I feel like myself again, like it's me, Clemens, standing there. I can feel that it's my heart that's beating, I can look down and see my own arm. I can tell that I'm here and that I'm separate from the mountains around me."

Halvorsen smiled at him.

"It's a tremendous feeling," Clemens said, smiling back. A smidge apologetically.

"It's damnation," Halvorsen said. "And what it feels like to exist, to be alive."

Halvorsen leaned over and started untying one of his boots. "Shoot, I didn't even notice until now that I haven't taken these off yet," he said, shaking his head.

Clemens smiled. "I'm sure a terrible stench will now pervade the room," Clemens joked.

"It may well," Halvorsen said, getting up and setting his boots off to the side a little. Then he went over to the fireplace.

"It's nice over here," he said. "Why don't we pull a couple of chairs over here?"

Clemens stood up. He couldn't remember the last time he'd had such a strong desire to talk as he did tonight. He moved quickly and eagerly, almost like a child, as he swung two armchairs over in front of the fire. It would be great to sit here, Halvorsen and him, he thought and sat down.

"Damnation occurs in the great works," Halvorsen said once he had taken a seat and arranged his feet in their grey ski socks on the hearth in front of the fireplace.

"What?" Clemens asked.

"Whenever I hear Bach's "Mass in B Minor" or "The Art of Fugue" or "The Musical Offering," or any other piece that speaks to me, I get that feeling you're talking about. That's damnation. I don't feel it when I hear Chopin."

He made a face, and Clemens started laughing.

"Chopin is talented. Chopin is brilliant and charming. That's all on the outside. But Bach has that extra something. Something sublime, or how else should I put it? He makes my heart beat faster."

"Just like when I'm up in the mountains?"

Halvorsen nodded.

"Exactly," he said. "And back when I was still playing…"

He put both his hands on his thighs and looked down at them.

"When I would practice a piece, it was like getting to know a landscape. I would find the paths that led through it, and I got to know where all the hills and valleys were. But I had to do something else too. I had to get to know it, the way you would get to know another person. Because unlike a landscape, the piece was created by a human being after all."

"You know, there are some who think the landscapes were created too," Clemens said, "by a god."

Halvorsen waved his hand dismissively.

"There is no God. And we don't need Him either. Some people call the kinds of experiences we're sitting here talking about right now religious experiences. I don't think they are. I think people are so full of feelings and sensations and we only notice them if we're open to them."

"But if it had been a religious experience," Clemens said, "if it had been a feeling of closeness to God, then maybe it wouldn't have felt so lonely."

Halvorsen looked at him but didn't say anything.

"Don't you think?" Clemens asked.

"I think you notice the loneliness because you feel those feelings only when you're up here," Halvorsen said, making a sweeping gesture with his arm to indicate the mountains. "Because you only feel that intensity in the mountains."

Clemens wrinkled his brow.

"Well, I feel it when I'm having sex, too," he admitted.

Halvorsen smiled at him.

"So, you feel helpless?"

Clemens nodded. "And very much alive," he said.

"But only when you're having sex?"

Clemens thought about it. Then he nodded again.

"Although I feel very confident when I'm having sex," he said.

For a while they just sat there staring into the flames, which had gradually burned down to flickering embers.

Then Halvorsen said, "I also feel it up here. In the fall I breathe the scent of mushrooms and of the decaying floor of the forest deep into my lungs. I love the solitude too. But there are also other things that can touch me and make me feel the intensity you feel in the mountains."

"Yeah?" Clemens said.

"Music. And people," Halvorsen said. "Even ones I'm not having sex with."

Clemens pulled his chair back from the fire a little. He'd rather talk about the mountains. That was what meant something to him.

"But of course that's more difficult," Halvorsen said. "People change and they do things you don't expect or don't understand."

"Yes!" Clemens said. "People do the strangest things."

"They certainly do. And they can make a man miserable."

Clemens sighed deeply.

"And sometimes it's just impossible to know how you're supposed to feel toward them," he said.

"You mean sometimes it's impossible to know how you do feel toward them," Halvorsen corrected him.

Clemens leaned forward and rested his forearms on his thighs while he peeled a piece of bark that had come off one of the birch logs next to the fireplace into strips.

"It's those women in Germany. I can't forget their faces. Their eyes were staring at me from eye sockets that were way too deep. And while the women were wandering around looking for people and things in the mounds of rubble, the children would just sit there listlessly in the middle of all the debris from the bombed out buildings. Other children were walking around all by themselves, crying, with their fingers in their mouths. I don't know what they were looking for."

"And what did you do?" Halvorsen asked.

"Well I…" Clemens said, "I hated them, the Germans. I mean, we hated them!"

His voice sounded desperate.

Halvorsen didn't say anything. And Clemens sat there feeling the weight of his words. How the words burned in him.

"When you're up in the mountains, you feel both small and large, and happy and horrified. Isn't that what you're saying?" Halvorsen said after a while.

Clemens nodded.

"There's plenty of space in you to make room for all of those feelings."

"There is?"

"So you can make room for the conflicting feelings you have toward people, too."

Clemens sat down. Did he really think it was a matter of *making room*? That sounded like some kind of ridiculous old-man mumbo-jumbo.

"So the whole thing comes down to what I can make room for?" he asked.

Clemens's voice was terse now.

"So it's not about what's bothering me? About the people who are doing this stuff to me? About the shitheads who hurt me? About the stinking, messed-up world we live in? You sound like some kind of sanctimonious old fart who just wants me to turn the other cheek!"

Clemens was disappointed. Profoundly disappointed. And he started to feel his chest tightening again. This time without the warmth that had been there before.

Halvorsen had gotten up. He was standing with his back to Clemens staring out one of the windows. Although it was almost midnight, there was a veil of light over the Hardanger Plateau.

"You've misunderstood me," he said.

"Unfortunately I don't think I have," Clemens said, rubbing his face with his hands.

They'd been sitting here drinking and talking all evening. And Clemens had felt energized and intoxicated. Both from the liquor and the emotion of it all. And in an instant it had all drained out of him, and he crumbled, as if whatever had been propping him up the whole evening had vanished.

"I don't mean that you should turn the other cheek," Halvorsen said, turning to face Clemens. "I just mean that there's no point in losing yourself in the loneliness *because* you're scared."

"What the hell is this?" Clemens yelled, jumping up. "Suddenly I'm just some quivering little coward? What the heck kind of nonsense is that? That's not *me* you're talking about. You don't know me!"

Clemens slammed the door behind him and ran to the bedroom. He considered waking Gustav up, but decided against it and started packing instead. They had to move on in the morning. They would head in toward Rembesdal even though they'd agreed to stay in Finse a few days. Gustav wouldn't mind. That's what they would do.

Everyone was sitting around the table eating breakfast when Clemens and Gustav walked in. Everyone except Halvorsen. And the anger drained out of Clemens the same way the happiness had, and he looked around the room with concern.

"Halvorsen?" he said out into the room.

"He left a good forty-five minutes ago," one of the Norwegian men said.

"More like half an hour ago," another said.

"Where did he go?"

"Toward Kjeldebu," said the woman who'd come in to put wood on the fire the night before.

Clemens nodded and rushed out the door. He was already on his way before she was finished speaking. Gustav started to get up, but Clemens hollered that he would be back. And then he ran off to put on his boots and parka. His fingers were shaking as he laced the boots.

"Damn it," he mumbled, leaping up.

There wasn't a living being in sight when he emerged from the cabin, no Halvorsen, not even a reindeer or a wood grouse. But once he jogged up to the top of a pile of rocks, he was able to see a small figure in knickers and a parka and with a light grey backpack bumping in against his back. He put his hands to his mouth and shouted, but the figure carried on indifferently down below. He ran down as quickly as he could without slipping on the loose rocks. Leaning slightly forward as he braced his one arm against the bigger boulders he passed on his way down. When he made it down and the path straightened out again, he sped up. It was strange that he could run and run and still never catch up to Halvorsen who was just walking, surely and steadily at a fixed, even pace.

"Halvorsen!" Clemens shouted.

And this time his voice echoed around the mountainsides with a "…sen, …sen, …sen," and when the first "…sen" hit Halvorsen, it was as if it spun him around so he was standing face to face with Clemens by the time the last "…sen" came back to him. And now Halvorsen stopped.

Clemens wasn't really out of breath when he got to him. But all the same his heart was pounding as if he'd climbed Norway's tallest mountain or run a marathon. Halvorsen didn't say anything. He just stood there in silence, waiting. Straight up and down with one arm down by his side and the other in under the shoulder strap of his backpack. He wasn't smiling, but didn't look angry either. If anything, he looked expectant.

Clemens inhaled as if he were about to say something, but nothing came out. No words formed between his lips, and he gave up and shut them again. As if he only had this one opportunity to form words and now he had forfeited it. He sagged a little watching Halvorsen with his eyes, which were sad and desperate at the same time. He didn't have much time. There were limits to how long he could keep Halvorsen here without having anything to say to him, because it didn't seem like Halvorsen wanted to talk. Not because he seemed angry or hurt, sooner because he had apparently already said everything he had to say.

Clemens wanted to fling himself at Halvorsen and beg him to stay. You can't leave, he wanted to say. Of course that would be crazy, but right now he felt like he wouldn't be able to bear the sight of Halvorsen disappearing around the next bend, and he opened his mouth again. But this time only a sigh came out, and he shook his head. It wasn't going to work. That's just how it was. But right then Halvorsen lifted his hand and stroked Clemens over the hair as if he were a little boy.

Then he turned around and walked on. And Clemens stood dumbfounded with his heart racing in his chest and watched the Swede getting smaller and smaller until he disappeared in a hollow.

Now there was only silence around Clemens. Halvorsen had disappeared into the mountainous terrain. Forever. And he had been so close. He could have said something, he could have gone with him. He could have gone with Halvorsen. They could have roamed together, the two of them. Kilometre after kilometre. They could have wandered the length and breadth of Norway. They could have been nomads. And Clemens would never have felt lonely or desperate again.

But he couldn't. He couldn't say anything. He couldn't reach out to Halvorsen, and on the way back to Finse, he felt a tinge of shame because Halvorsen had stroked him over the hair like that.

ৡ Clemens sat down in the canvas chair. He ran one of his hands restlessly over his thigh. Then he jumped up again. This must've been the tenth time he'd jumped up out of the chair. Peter looked at him out of the corner of his eye before he bent back over his work again.

"Is your watch right, Peter?" Clemens asked, trying to force his voice to sound casual.

Peter nodded, looking at it.

"It's ten after seven," he said.

Clemens looked at his own watch.

"Yes," he said. "It's ten after seven."

Peter nodded.

"Weren't they supposed to be back by four?"

"Yeah," Peter said.

"Yeah," Clemens said, leaving the tent area.

He walked quickly, stumbling slightly, up to the top of the seif dune that was on the east side of camp. He scanned the eastern horizon. And he had been up there numerous times since five o'clock. And there still wasn't anything to see.

Peter stood up and started coming over to him. Not quickly and restlessly like Clemens. Peter stood at the foot of the seif with his hands in his pockets and looked up at Clemens as he started coming down.

Clemens shook his head.

"I can't see them," he said, looking at his watch.

"No," Peter said.

"We're going to have to drive out there after them," Clemens said, painstakingly avoiding looking Peter in the eye.

Peter nodded. He knew that if Anna hadn't gone, there was no way Clemens would be driving out there like this. He would have waited much longer. But Peter nodded and gathered his papers together. Meanwhile Clemens packed lamps and water and made sure that the spare tank was full of gas, that the toolbox was where it should be, and that the signal flares were under the front seat. Then he hopped into the Jeep and started driving slowly out of the camp. He leaned over the passenger's seat and pushed the door open as he got to Peter.

They'd been gone since six in the morning, Leo and Anna, and they should've been back by four in the afternoon, by five at the latest, and now it was almost seven thirty.

Clemens and Peter headed east, but after driving for an hour, they changed course and headed north by northwest. Leo and Anna wouldn't be so far east.

"They must've gone north," Clemens said, looking at Peter who was sitting there with one boot up on the dashboard.

"Yup," he said, "they probably drove further north. We'll run into them soon."

"If only I'd sent Sayeed with them," Clemens muttered.

Peter looked over at him. Then he looked startled.

"Look over there, Clemens," he said.

Clemens looked out the side window, diagonally behind them. And there was an enormous wave of sand hanging in the yellow air, quivering. Clemens slowed down and now he was able to see what he already knew full well: that it wasn't hanging there motionless, but pummeling ahead at uncontrollable speed. It was the khamsin. They both knew it. In a flash, Clemens positioned the Jeep as much in the lee of a sand bank as he could and then they ran around to the tailgate and grabbed what they would need in the way of water and scarves. After that they ran back around, got into the car, rolled up the windows and shut the doors. They wound the scarves around their faces so that only slits were left for their eyes, because the sand would find its way in no matter how well they sealed everything up.

By two thirty the sandstorm had moved on and a starry black sky opened up over them. They managed to push open the door on Peter's side and Clemens ran up the nearest peak and scanned the desert for the other Jeep. It would be easy for him to spot their emergency flare now, so all he had to do was watch and wait.

Meanwhile Peter found the shovel and started digging out the Jeep. The sand had buried the hood, the windshield, and the front part of the roof. The rest was pretty much untouched. And after half an hour he was able to join Clemens who was pacing back and forth, alternately staring first one way then the other. But by five in the morning they still hadn't seen anything, and Clemens could feel how his hands were beginning to tremble. Peter placed his hand on Clemens's head, pulling him in closer. Just a little.

"They may already be back in camp," Clemens said.

They got back to camp at eight. But the other Jeep wasn't there. Clemens ran out of the Jeep yelling for Sayeed. He found him behind one of the tents where he was squatting, drawing in the sand with his fingers.

"I'm asking the sand," he said, looking up at Clemens.

He drew two fingers through the sand so that there was a set of parallel grooves. Then he hit the sand between the grooves with his knuckles. Quickly and unerringly so they formed little depressions. He counted the depressions and the groves and then looked up at Clemens.

"They're coming," he said, grinning with his wide mouth that was missing the five front teeth on the top. "They're coming, boss!"

Clemens couldn't help but feel relieved. He ran both hands through his hair.

"Can you see when?" he asked.

"Soon."

"Soon," Clemens muttered, turning around and going into his tent.

Just about an hour later the Jeep pulled into camp. Clemens ran out and opened the door on Anna's side before Leo had even come to a stop. He pulled her out of the car and hugged her to him while he glared angrily at Leo who'd just climbed out of the car.

Leo flung out his arms apologetically.

"Please don't be mad, Clemens," he said.

Peter stood in the background, watching.

"I know, it's not good, but I darn well lost my bearings," Leo said. "And then on top of it all there was that awful sandstorm."

"You can't fucking lose your bearings out here, Leo!" Clemens said.

His voice was ice cold and shaky.

Leo sighed and flung out his arms again.

"Why didn't you light the emergency flares?" Clemens asked. "We scanned for them for over two hours, Peter and me."

Anna looked from the one to the other. Her face and hair were grey with sand.

"We didn't have any," Leo said.

Clemens took a step toward him.

"You didn't have any emergency flares?" he said.

"I hadn't checked."

Now Clemens yelled.

"What the fuck is wrong with you! You drove out there without checking your emergency flares? That's the most irresponsible thing I've ever heard of!"

Then he took a deep breath.

"I have yet to see what you can do," Clemens said.

Then he turned around and walked over to his tent, kicking up clouds of sand.

Anna ran after him, and Peter turned around to head into his tent and go to sleep. But Leo just stood there. The muscles in his jaws were flexing beneath the skin. Then he tuned and kicked the base of the seif with all his might, roaring. Not any words, just an inarticulate sound.

EL-KHÂRGA, NOVEMBER 1996

☙ I feel awful admitting it, the feeling has been creeping up on me, maybe because I'm so far away and ripped out of my normal everyday life, but I'm enjoying it, actually, I'm actually enjoying taking a break from Mette for a little while. I mean, obviously I'm going to miss her, but right now I'm breathing freer.

I've been daydreaming, just sort of idling, sometimes there's nothing going on inside me, other times I drift off and just stand there staring into space, and then feelings come to the surface, a tickling sensation in my stomach or the feeling that my heart has skipped a beat.

Mette is a very capable woman, she's strong and decisive, plop her down in some new and unfamiliar location and she'll get her bearings in a flash and have a sense of what the norms are there, and then she'll join right in. She doesn't just adapt, she takes charge, efficiently and energetically. Completely different from me, I'm somewhat slow at it, I drift off to other places, or just don't quite fit in.

Mette's a librarian, I met her at the library on Dag Hammarskjölds Allé where she worked back then, that was ten years ago, and I was only twenty-five. I was wandering around like I usually do, just sort of foraging through the stacks, a little in the fiction section, a little in poetry, and a little in travel books, and then she came over and asked if she could help me find anything, or something like that, and I was a little surprised, I mean, it's not like I was in a clothing store or something, but she smiled so sweetly and cocked her head to the side, and so did I, and so we stood that way for a little while, with our faces tilted to the side, until I started laughing, and then she looked at me questioningly, "No, thanks," I said, "I'm just foraging around." "Foraging?" she said, looking around her. "We don't really have any nuts or berries here,"

101

then of course I smiled again. Then I said, "I'm not really looking for anything specific." "I see," she said, peeking curiously at the book I was holding, it was Thorkild Bjørnvig or Thorkild Hansen, or maybe it was the *Rough Guide to the Algarve*.

To be honest, I don't remember at all. "Oh," she said, nodding approvingly, so it must not have been the *Rough Guide to Algarve*, it must have been Thorkild Bjørnvig, but it could also have been Schade or even Schwitters, I might have been standing there with the "Anna Blossom" poem, now wouldn't that have been ironic? But I wasn't. I was just standing there with Hans-Jørgen Nielsen's *The Soccer Angel*, mostly because I've always really liked the cover with that soccer player's butt on it.

It wasn't long before I moved in with Mette, into her apartment, a one-bedroom where everything had its place and every place had a thing: bathroom scale, hand-held mixer, designer flower pots, springform pans, Q-Tips, and Bag Balm, everything, even washcloths, she must have had at least thirty-five washcloths. And I was just getting by with a dishcloth, a clean one, of course, and there I was in my ratty sneakers not knowing what to do with my hands, so I just ran them through my hair, until she came and took them and pulled me down on top of her on the bed.

She would just suddenly take charge of the situation that way. Then she would peel off my clothes and whisper all kinds of things in my ear: that she loved me, that I looked good, hot, had an amazing butt... But I never really managed to whisper anything back.

And then she wanted to meet my parents, so we took the light rail line up to Lyngby out to their house, and I suppose that's where she made up her mind for real, because I come from a very cultured home: functionalism and Børge Mogensen, and books and hand-woven carpets and tea and orange marmalade, never jelly. And Thora's finished and half-finished paintings and my father's rocks, it's never been neat, not that neat anyway. And my father. He was there too of course, and the ladies have always liked him, they think he's very masculine, and then there's apparently something about his eyes, they say they're very intense. Women love that kind of thing.

Mette thinks I look a lot like him. "You're good-looking men, the two of you," she says. "How lucky for me that I got mixed up with this family."

ॐ They took their last exams yesterday and now it was summer vacation. Clemens was standing in Busck's Bookstore, poking around in the sale bins. He was going to go home to Viborg tomorrow, but today he would meet Gustav at three o'clock at the restaurant Tokanten to celebrate the beginning of vacation.

There weren't that many people in the bookstore, because the weather was nice and most people were lounging around in the parks enjoying the sun, so Clemens quickly noticed the young man who was covetously surveying the store, scanning first one shelf then another.

He was thin and lanky, and his hair – which was actually unusually thin – was sticking up wildly in the air because he was continually running his hand through it and rumpling it. He was wearing a plaid lumberjack shirt, rolled up well above the elbows, and a wide leather belt was holding his pants up. Despite the clothes, he didn't look very outdoorsy. He was way too delicate and awkward in his movements. And his face was too pale and fine.

But he was astonishingly sure in his opinions, Clemens could hear. These books were a bunch of inconsequential drivel, those were a bunch of hooey, but this one here, this was the real thing.

"Paul La Cour. I'm sick of him!" the man exclaimed.

Clemens craned his neck to see who the man was talking to. It was a young woman. She was wearing a light blue houndstooth check dress with short sleeves and a pleated skirt. As was all the rage with them these days, the girls. But she wasn't chic like so many of the others. Not that she was ungainly. It wasn't like that. Her movements were precise.

Then she hit the man over the head with a book. Clemens smiled. That'll show him, he thought. But he couldn't figure out what was keeping her from

103

being stylish. Then he realized what it was. It was her hair. It wasn't done up like the other girls'. It was just cut off at chin length, and it didn't have any wave or curl to it. It was thick and bristly. And her face was more self-assured and more obstinate than he was used to seeing on a girl; her mouth was broad, her nose was broad, and her eyebrows were too. Dark brown and broad. Her face was actually much coarser than his own.

The guy was back at it again. Now he was poopooing Thorkild Bjørnvig, as far as Clemens could hear. But then she raised her purse and set it on one of the bookshelves, pressed the metal clasp down and flipped up the leather flap. The guy kept talking the whole time, but it was obvious that she wasn't paying attention, she was rummaging around looking for something. Then Clemens could see that she'd found whatever it was she was looking for. But he couldn't tell what it was, until she brought the thing up to her mouth and blew it right in the guy's ear. It was a harmonica. Clemens smiled, shaking his head. Then he walked over to the counter to pay for the book he'd selected. It was A Farewell to Arms, and it was on sale for only 3.75 kroner.

As he walked past them, he turned his head slightly and smiled at her in approval. Rather furtively. He hadn't expected the guy to notice.

"Hey, buddy," he called after Clemens. "We're sure having a blast here, huh?"

Clemens could hear from his voice that he wasn't angry. But he couldn't decide if the guy was irritated or having a good time. It seemed like everyone was in such a good mood today.

Clemens turned around, went over to the guy, and held out his hand to him; he said his name was Josef and that he wasn't a Jew despite the name and the nose.

"My mother had just painted a picture of Joseph when she had me. And she thought it was so wonderful how he walked beside that donkey… or whatever it was," he said quickly, shaking his head apologetically.

Clemens smiled. Could you have a mother who painted pictures? The idea struck him as absurd.

"And now I have to do the whole shtick every time I meet someone new," he said.

Then he put his hand on the girl's shoulder and said she was his cousin, Anna. And then he apologized that she always caused such a ruckus with her harmonica.

Clemens grinned and flung out his arms.

"It's a good thing you've got that," he said to Anna, nodding at the harmonica in her hand.

He grinned at Josef, whose tall body swayed a little as he was clearly searching for a snappy retort. His eyes seemed unusually intelligent and animated, Clemens thought, though he never did come up with that retort.

Anna looked at Clemens. Her lips moved a little. Not as if she were going to say something. They just moved. But her eyes didn't move. They were looking straight into his. What was going on here? Apparently nothing, because now she was staring at the cookbooks on the shelf to her left. She pulled one out and started flipping through it. And Josef was talking. Clemens didn't hear what he was saying, because he was watching her. A – N – N – A, he heard in his head. She was like a magnet, he couldn't take his eyes off her. A drop of sweat slid down his armpit. It was so hot that day. His eyes were like a nail, caught in her magnetic force, and he followed the outline of her neck and further down. Josef flung out his hands, shook his head and walked over to a different bookshelf. Anna set the cookbook on a shelf full of novels and pulled out Tarjei Vesaas's *The Bridges*.

"This one is supposed to be good," she said.

Clemens didn't respond.

"Well, that's what I've heard anyway," she mumbled, putting the book back.

Then she glanced up at him and this time she didn't look away. They were in that place where you don't say "hi" or "what lovely weather we're having" or "this is supposed to be a good book," but where everything softens and your lungs turn into a big pump, hard at work breathing somewhere in your body, and you're powerless.

What should he do? He was thinking fast now, because just standing there and asking her for her address was totally out of the question. He didn't even know her. But what if he never saw her again? He wrinkled his brow. She did too. He smiled at her, and she smiled back.

"I suppose you guys are going to the party at Regensen Hall on Friday?" he said then.

It was a shot in the dark. He'd been invited, but had said he couldn't make it because he wanted to go home and help out in the fields at the agricultural college, go home and breathe the fresh air.

"Yeah," she said, nodding. "We are, actually. Or *I* am. I mean, Josef isn't."

Clemens took a deep breath.

"Well then I'm sure we'll see each other there," he said in a voice that was way too eager, and he reached out to shake her hand goodbye and started walking backward while he hollered goodbye to Josef, who was squatting in front of the poetry shelf and just waved his hand in response.

 The light from the campfire turned Sayeed's face golden, and when he tilted his head back, roaring in laughter, his mouth became a black hole in the middle of his face. Leo was telling jokes and he winked at Anna while Sayeed was laughing so hard that he was stomping his feet in the sand. Anna looked down. She didn't like the way he treated Sayeed. But she often had a hard time keeping herself from laughing because he really was funny, that Leo. And it felt liberating, out here in this bleak ocean of sand, just to give in to the laughter and the whiskey, which Leo poured so liberally.

Clemens and Peter had driven to Mût the day before. They were going to have trouble with the authorities if they didn't get their papers stamped there. And besides, soon they would be running short on gas and water and several other necessities. It would be another three days before they came back.

Clemens had really wanted Anna to come, but she needed to get away from his seriousness. She needed to have a good time. And Leo had promised Clemens he'd take good care of her. But it hadn't seemed like Clemens had all that much faith in that. True, Leo could be a little rash, she would certainly grant Clemens that, but surely he wasn't anywhere near as bad as Clemens made him out to be. They were just opposites, the two of them, she thought. Clemens was professional and responsible, Leo just kind of fudged his way through and didn't think about things so much in advance, because everything would work out in the end, that's obviously what he thought. Clemens was the grown man, Leo the wild adolescent boy. Yes, that was just how it was, she thought. Leo saw Clemens as a father figure, one he was always rebelling against. She smiled at the thought. There probably wasn't anything more to it than that, and it actually made Leo quite cute, she thought. And harmless.

She'd been attracted to him the whole time, she was aware of that. He

had this wildness, this brashness. But she had allowed Clemens's dislike of
him to influence her. Clemens must have good reasons, she had thought.
There must really be something rotten about Leo, the way Clemens distanced
himself from him. But now it occurred to her that Clemens ought to be
strong enough to just suck it up and take whatever rebellion Leo dished out.
He was the expedition leader, after all, and was supposed to have a thick skin.
And besides she was tired of all his seriousness and incessant work. People
needed to have a little fun now and then, didn't they?

Sayeed stood up to go to bed, and Anna held out her cup and Leo filled
it. She drank, almost as if it were tea he had given her, and when she took the
cup away from her lips, the fire was swaying, and Leo seemed to be rocking
back and forth in front of her. It didn't feel unpleasant, more mellow and
peaceful really. As if she were sitting in a boat gently rocking on the sea and
could just lie back and enjoy the soothing motions, confident that the boat
would sail her along to wherever she was supposed to be going. She didn't
need to do anything. She could just let herself drift along with the current.

And that was what she did when Leo leaned over her and kissed her. It
had been many years since she had been kissed by a man other than Clemens,
and it felt unreal. As if it were Clemens she was kissing, but the whole scene
was somehow distorted and strange. Like a photograph that was double-
exposed.

Leo nestled in against her and ran his hands through her hair. She pulled
his shirt up out of his pants and reached her hands in over his naked back. It
wasn't as long as Clemens's.

Anna simultaneously felt an intense desire for Leo and a strangeness.
When she would lean into Clemens, she just fell into place. That didn't
happen to her here with Leo. And that created a sinking feeling of insecurity
in her stomach, but there was more lust. She wanted Leo, she lusted after this
man who desired her as intensely as she knew he did.

Three days went by before Clemens and Peter came back. In that time, Anna
practically hadn't left her tent. She had slept a lot and every time she was
about to wake up, she tried hard to fall asleep again. During the day it was
blisteringly hot in the tent, and when she woke up she would be dripping
with sweat, her hair greasy, and she would peel her shirt off and throw it
down onto the groundsheet that served as the floor. If she wasn't sleeping,
she was writing in her book, which was looking thicker and thicker the more
she wrote in it, as if the letters and words were swelling it up, but in reality it
was surely just the sweat from her hands and the grains of sand that made the
pages wavy and thick.

And then they finally came, Clemens and Peter, and she pressed herself against Clemens when he climbed out of the Jeep. They had gotten along well together, she could tell. Peter looked happier and more relaxed. As if he had moved his face more than usual, as if he had talked more. And Clemens seemed happy to see her.

"Did things go well?" he asked, studying her face.

"Yes," she whispered.

"Where's Leo?" he asked.

She turned around, and right then he came sauntering out of his tent. She looked at him, alert but unable to figure out what he was going to do, how he would react to Clemens. She didn't know him anywhere near well enough to predict.

He nodded to Clemens.

"Well, we're back," Clemens said, trying to make his voice sound upbeat.

He stared at Leo inquisitively and for far too long.

Then Leo cocked his head a little, gave him a mocking look, and then winked at Anna. Quickly and almost imperceptibly.

Clemens pushed Anna aside and lunged at him, planting a clenched fist into the side of his head. Leo didn't duck in time and clutched his cheek in surprise, and then he flung himself on Clemens.

Anna screamed. She'd never seen people move so quickly and violently. She hadn't imagined it was possible. Clemens and Leo weren't men anymore – they were animals, she thought. Or maybe they were just men. Anna felt hot; at the same time she was shocked and scared.

Peter was already bending over them where they were lying in the sand, and Sayeed had come running. Together the two men managed to pull them off each other. And when they got up again, their faces were streaked with sweat and sand, and their bodies were ready to pounce. Their breathing was jerky and much too rapid. They seemed alien and unnerving, Anna thought when she went over to Clemens and held him. He was soaking wet, and his skin was bright red down over his chest.

"Come on," she said, pulling him along.

Under the awning from the tent she took his clothes off and bathed him with water from one of the plastic drums. She didn't say anything and neither did he. But she could tell that the water she was pouring over him felt good.

"I love you," she whispered.

"It doesn't feel like it," he said.

She dropped her arms and the water container.

NORTHEAST OF THE GILF EL-KEBÎR, OCTOBER 1958

They say that when a group of people travels through the desert, the sheep and goats die first. They can survive only for a few days without water. Then the children die, then the women. There isn't time to stop for each death because then it would just take even longer to reach the well, and one death would end up causing another.

The men and the camels live for a while longer. Camels can survive without water for three weeks, and in that time they can walk five hundred kilometres. During these weeks, female camels have a small amount of milk in their udders. And the man knows that this is how long he has to find water.

After that, the camel's udder is empty and cracked, and they die together. The man and the camel.

The heat is monstrous. And the air is dry. All you can smell here is the dryness. Dust and dryness. And the heat and the dryness make it almost impossible to breathe the air down into your lungs.

We've been here six months, and we have two left. I'm starting to find myself wishing it were over.

CC, latitude 24° north, longitude 27° east. October 10, 1958

  Anna was having trouble sleeping. Her body wouldn't stay on the mattress. It wasn't heavy enough, constantly threatening to float up into the air. And not in a pleasant way. Rather, it filled her with a terrifying helplessness. No matter how heavy she tried to make herself, no matter how much she tried to press her body back into the restful relaxation, it had this keyed-up lightness, and her efforts were useless.

Moreover she felt that her soul had been shattered into a myriad of sand grains, small glittering sand grains, lying like a porous coating between her skin and her bones. Every time she moved, the grains slid back and forth, scoring the top of her bones and the underside of her skin.

No one talked about what had happened. Come to think of it, no one talked about much of anything. For a long time. Peter worked assiduously and doggedly. Leo had suddenly driven off in one of the Jeeps and didn't come back until four days later. Clemens suspected he'd been in El-Khârga, but no one knew for sure, and Leo didn't say anything. Otherwise Leo alternated between exploding with bursts of enthusiasm and shutting himself in his tent, where he could sleep until late into the day. In the evenings he dedicated himself to drinking.

Clemens was the quietest of them all. In the mornings he would drive off in one of the Jeeps and in the middle of the day he would come back to eat. After the meal, during the hottest hours, he would sit at the table and continue working on the observations he had made that morning, and on the samples he had collected.

He would never dream of sending Leo home. That would be the same as acknowledging that he couldn't handle his duties as expedition leader. The

110

man who holds the group together and keeps everyone's spirits up even at the most difficult times. So, for Clemens the most important thing was trying to stick to the routines that they had established long ago.

He didn't talk to Anna much either. She mostly sat at her desk and wrote in her book. He had no idea what she was writing, but assumed she was working on various medical problems.

COPENHAGEN, JUNE 1952

๛ Clemens managed to turn his 'no' to the party invitation into a yes. The
hardest part had been having to call his mother to say he would be late, that he
wouldn't arrive until four days later. But here he was, sitting in the Great Hall
in Regensen, one of the oldest student dorms in Copenhagen. Anna was there,
he had noted that ages ago, but he hadn't talked to her yet. She was sitting all
the way down at the end of the hall. Between a redheaded guy and Gustav,
who it turned out she vaguely knew from somewhere. Must be something
about Anna's and Gustav's fathers being colleagues. Clemens hadn't quite
figured out how everything fit together, but he had just seen Gustav make a
funny face and had heard him whispering that Anna obviously wasn't quite
all there. And that he had heard that Anna's mother was supposed to have
been completely insane, that's what Gustav's father said anyway. But then it
didn't take much for Gustav to think people weren't quite all there. He could
be terribly intolerant, Clemens thought, so he just shot him an angry look and
found a spot between two girls he knew from the Geology Department.

Then the evening had worn on, although to Clemens it felt like time was
standing still. They ate and got through some of the numerous boring rituals
they were so fond of here at Regensen. But when the room started to smell
stale, like leftover beer and cigarette smoke, most of the group went down to
the Small Hall to dance. Clemens looked around for Anna, and there she was.
Sitting in the farthest corner. Sitting up straight on a flimsy chair with her
harmonica in her hands. Her hair had fallen down over her face, and behind
it she was holding onto the harmonica with her broad hands. Her eyes were
closed.

Clemens walked over to her.

"Anna," he said.

112

There was a brief lull in the notes from the harmonica, a melody that sounded like it came from somewhere in the Balkans. Then they started up again.

He squatted down in front of her.

"Clemens!" someone said from over at the table. "Leave her alone."

It was Gustav. Now he was standing up. Clemens turned his head and looked at him. Gustav gestured that he should come back toward him. Clemens turned toward Anna again.

"Anna," he repeated quietly, insistently. "You are from behind as from in front."

Slowly she opened her eyes and looked down at him. Heavily. The notes diminished in intensity and sounded more and more peculiar. Like the dry winds in the Carpathians.

"Who are you, uncounted broad, you are, are you?
People say you'd be.
Let them say it, they don't know how the steeple's standing.
You're wearing your hat on your feet, wandering on your hands."

Clemens could see that she was smiling behind the harmonica.

He smiled too.

"A – N – N – A! I drizzle your name.
Your name drips like tallow.
Do you, Anna, you do know,
People can read you even from behind."

Anna cocked one eyebrow. Her eyes twinkled.

"And you, the most splendid of all,
You are from behind as from in front: A – N – N – A.
CARESSING drizzles tallow over my back.
Anna Blossom, you drippy beast,"

"Clemens!" Gustav yelled.

"I – love – your!" Clemens whispered

Anna closed her eyes and blew sound like a howling wind out of the harmonica.

"Clemens! God damn it!"

It was Gustav.

He was standing over by the table. On the other side of it.

Clemens took hold of Anna's arm and pulled her up out of the chair.

"Come on!" he said.

She followed him reluctantly, but he pulled harder on her, and finally she had to jog to keep up with him down the stairs.

Soon they were standing on the street below, Store Kannikestræde. In the rain. Clemens pushed her in against the wall of the building. The rain was streaming over them. Her hair lay like drenched twine around her neck and down her face. Her eyes were fixed on his. Clemens's eyes got darker and darker. He pressed his thumb in behind her teeth and felt how wet and warm it was in there.

At that instant, Gustav came around the corner down the street.

"What the hell," Clemens swore, "what is that lunkhead doing?"

A car sped by and splashed water up onto the bottom of Gustav's coat.

"Hey!" he yelled, clenching his fist after the car.

Clemens grabbed Anna's arm and pulled her along with him.

"Clemens!" Gustav yelled. "Leave her alone."

"Shut up, Gustav!" Clemens yelled back.

Anna reached for Clemens's hand. They jumped over puddles that glistened metallically under the streetlights and zigzagged in and out between the umbrellas and men and women hurrying along with their collars up around their ears or briefcases over their heads.

When they got to Anna's apartment on Larslejsstræde, water was streaming over their faces and clothes, and their shoes were soaked. They took all their clothes off and hung most of them over the back of a chair by the oil stove in the corner. They put the rest on a couple of clothes hangers they hung on two hooks in the ceiling.

The rain and all the wet clothing made the situation simple. No shyness, no hesitation. And it wasn't until they were standing there facing each other, naked, that they realized they were standing there. Naked. The cold and the wet clothing had left red waves on their skin, and Anna's lips were pale. She shivered and trembled a little. But other than that she didn't move. Without hiding it, she stared at Clemens. Examining him closely. She was observing him as if he were a specimen, an anatomical model. The shoulders, the chest, the stomach, the groin, the genitals, the thighs, the legs, the feet. And he did the same to her. She was strong, he could see that, and stocky, but, oh, how amazingly beautiful. She had breasts and hips and thighs, she was curvaceous and unendurably womanly. He needed to see the inner sides of her thighs. She had to lie down in front of him and spread them apart so he could see how they thickened as they relaxed against the mattress.

He went to her, and in a single motion, spun her around so he could see the swell of her ass, and he knew that was what he had to do. See her ass.

Clemens was kneeling on the bed. His thighs apart. They seemed enormous, his thighs and knees, as he knelt there. The muscles were almost as pronounced as in those anatomical plates in her books. And she had studied the male anatomy so many times, the way the muscles stretched over the bones like leathery ropes, the bones that were so much larger than in the female model on the opposite page. The knee was larger, the shoulder, the forearm, the hand. Just the fact that everything was larger, made her wet. And now he grabbed hold of her hips with his hands and lifted them so she was resting against his thighs and her crotch was pointed up at him. All of his movements were sure and hungry without being fierce. He was thorough, Clemens was, and able to lose himself completely in what he was working on, whether it was a landscape or a woman. One could get lost in both. It didn't matter if he was standing high up on the Hardanger Plateau in Norway, inhaling the crisp, icy air over the eternal snow, or if he was down on his knees, gazing at a woman's crotch. He vanished, and yet such intense changes were taking place before his eyes: her labia were unfurling and glistening more and more merely from his gaze. His erection rose urgently, pressing against his stomach so he could feel the warmth and moistness of it against his skin. He didn't feel present, and yet he had caused such a marvelous transformation.

He felt the heat washing through his body with his blood. He felt its strength and desire and everything he could do with it. This body. And then he saw the woman squirming beneath him, and he heard her breathing and knew that she was yearning. He didn't think she was yearning for him, just that she was yearning, and he never had any doubt that he could satisfy her yearning just by satisfying his own. It was that simple.

He lay down between Anna's thighs and studied her vulva. For a long time he did not touch it, and she raised her head and looked down at him, and perhaps he lifted his face and met her gaze with eyes that were intense with curbed desire: a gravity and a will she'd never known before.

Anna loved Clemens. She gave herself to him completely. She'd read Sartre, Anna had, but she had no choice here.

EL-KHÂRGA, NOVEMBER 1996

❧ I ran into her again this morning, down in the bar, the woman who doesn't write.

Not that I do either, I mean, obviously I write when I write here in the hotel, but it's not like I'm sitting around writing and writing, one page after another, I just sit there. And that's what she does too.

She sits and stares straight ahead. I generally look at something, like her for example. But she looks at nothing, I can tell that, and this morning I could see that the sore on her heel was doing a little better, I think she cleaned it, it seemed dry and healthy, but a Band-Aid would certainly be appropriate.

I've never seen anyone sit as still as her, this morning she was leaning back with one hand in her lap and the other on the table, and nothing moved, the whole time I was sitting there watching her, she didn't move so much as a pinky toe, but there was something moving, I suddenly noticed it, it was a bead of sweat at the nape of her neck, below her pony tail, it sparkled, and at a certain point it started to slide down her neck until it disappeared under the collar on her dress, and after that new drops appeared, one after another, not that she turned into a leaking faucet, not at all, this all happened infinitely slowly, but the motion itself was intense.

I love women. It sounds dumb to say it like that, of course all men love women, but all the same I still think I'm entitled to say it, it says something about me, because I'm always really aware of women, even if they're not there, I'm aware of the vibration, the heat, the arousal; it's not necessarily the need to penetrate a woman but, rather, it's a sense of something filling *me*. That's how it was for my dad too, that's what I think, that's how I'm able to understand him.

"I think I have a Band-Aid I can give you." I was astonished to realize that I'd stood up and was standing there talking to her, I nodded at her heel, "A Band-Aid would be good, now that you've cleaned it, your sore, dirt will get into it so easily, especially here with the sand," she was staring up at me, I wasn't sure she saw me, or understood me, after all it was highly unlikely that she was also Danish. The look in her eyes didn't change, her lips seemed a little more expressive, "You should put a Band-Aid on," I said, nodding, this time not at her heel, now it was mostly to emphasize the importance of the Band-Aid, "It's important," I said.

She was still staring at me, and now her lips started to move, as if she wanted to say something, I leaned in toward her, "What's your name?" she whispered, in Danish. Her lips seemed so dry. "Are you thirsty?" I asked, leaning even further toward her. "What's your name?" she whispered again. I'd forgotten that she'd asked me something. "Tore," I said. "Tore," she whispered, and it was almost as if she were smiling, or else she was somehow in pain. "Are you in pain?" I asked. She nodded. "Where?" I asked and she pointed at her stomach. "My stomach hurts," she whispered.

And then she got up, but she didn't make it all the way up before she collapsed, thank God I just managed to grab hold of her, awfully clumsily, she was draped over me and felt heavy even though she was quite thin, but this limp body was totally unwieldy and it felt wrong standing there with the body of a woman I didn't know at all. The men were looking at me and I lifted her up so she was almost hanging over my shoulder, they were staring at me, the men, and I felt self-conscious and tried to set her back down on the floor so I could get a better hold, and finally I succeeded, I got one arm in under her knees and the other in under the back of her neck, it was damp, obviously. I'd already noticed that.

With my shoulder I managed to push open the door to the medical clinic, the heat pressed on my chest, and she felt heavy, heavier and heavier every step I took up the stone staircase, and she was pale, but she was breathing calmly and regularly.

I set her down on an examining table and it wasn't long until the doctor came. He pressed two fingers against her wrist, keeping his eye on his watch, after which he pulled up her eyelids and shined a small, bright light into each of her eyes. "Her stomach hurts," I said, and he nodded, pulled her dress up and started pressing on her abdomen. I felt warm, but he, a very young man, didn't even seem notice that the patient lying in front of him was a woman, his eyes were businesslike while his hands worked their way over her abdomen pressing on selected spots. He was touching her intestines. Not the skin on her belly.

That's how I want to be. But I'll never be like that.

"It's nothing serious," he said, straightening out her dress again. "She's just dehydrated." "But her stomach?" I asked. "There's nothing wrong with her," he said, inserting an IV into her right hand. And a nurse hooked a bag of saline solution onto a rack and attached the plastic tube from the bag to the drip in the woman's hand. Then they left the room and I sat down on a chair next to the examining table.

Her cheeks started to get some colour and her breathing got heavier, now she was just sleeping, the hand with the drip was lying on the sheet in front of me, it seemed like it had been mistreated lying there, thin, with its design of blue veins, and the skin pierced by the needle, I had to stop myself from pulling it out, and to distract myself I started watching the drops as they emerged from the bag of saline solution up there until they slid through the tube and disappeared into the needle and then into her body. She was drinking now. Through her skin. And that was good, I tried to tell myself.

The nurse came back with some papers for me to fill out. "Just write your wife's name there," she said, pointing at a box on the top page with the tip of a ballpoint pen. "Um, but, she's not my wife," I was about to say, I don't know how much I managed to get out, maybe I just said, "um, but" and fidgeted nervously, and then I took the paper and the pen and I had no idea what I should write, the nurse disappeared out the door again, and I watched the woman, her lips were beginning to get some colour, and it was as if they were filling up, "I don't know her name," I mumbled, but of course the nurse was already gone, and I suppose it didn't matter anyway, it was just a name after all, darn it, they just wanted a name on the form, and so I wrote Ane Carlsen.

I must've dozed off on that hard chair, because it was starting to get dark when she said my name. "Tore," she said. I sat up, I'm sure I'd been sitting all slovenly and slumped over, and maybe I was drooling, I reached for my mouth, she smiled. "You weren't drooling," she said, I cleared my throat, my mouth was dry, and I looked around for some water. "It's weird," she said quietly, "when men sleep they do different things with their arms than women do. If they lie down, they put their arms behind their head, and if they're sleeping sitting up, they fold their arms." She smiled. But even if she looked healthier, she still seemed weak.

"I didn't know what to write when they asked me to write down your name," I said. "So, what did you do?" "I wrote Ane," I said, "and then Carlsen, that's my last name." "Ane?" she said. "Yes," I said. "Ane," she repeated, "but that's not my name," she said, smiling, "just think if you'd guessed right!" I smiled.

"My name's Helga," she said after a bit. "Helga?" I asked. "Yes," she said. "Who's Ane?" I smiled. "That was my father's first great love." "Your father's?

I thought it was yours." I shook my head. "No, it wasn't mine."

She was lying in my bed in my room at the Trans-Saharan Hotel, and she was much healthier now and really wanted to eat, so I gave her oranges and dates whose skin I peeled off, I was afraid of bacteria, since she was so weak now, but first I'd flown around the room trying to tidy up: I'd gathered up my clothes from the floor and stuffed them into the closet, and I'd gathered the papers and letters and photographs into piles on the desk. And I'd switched off my cell phone. She saw me do that and I shrugged. "People can always just leave me a message," I said. "Are you married?" she asked. That startled me. "No," I said, almost before she'd finished asking the question. "Yes, I'm married." I was still standing there with the phone in my hand, so I turned it on and set it down on the desk, I sighed. "My wife's name is Mette," I said. "Her name isn't Ane?" I shook my head. "Mette," I said. "Do you love her?" "No," I said, and just like that my body felt heavy, infinitely heavy and tired, and I sat down and rubbed my forehead, what was I saying? My face was burning hot, and I looked over at Helga on the bed, her face was very sombre, and she didn't look like she wanted to say anything else.

"*My* husband is dead," she said, looking me right in the eye. I sat up in the chair and wanted to cry, which was completely inappropriate, I suppose, but those big eyes, they were so full of sorrow and yet so composed, she had a seriousness about her that seemed strange on such a young face. And then there were those red sandals.

My voice was all choked-up, I could easily hear that when I asked her about it. "It'll be a year," she said, "in three days, he had stomach cancer, and it spread, it ate him up from the inside, but he didn't want to accept it and he rushed along from one place to the next, we traveled until he got so sick that we plunked ourselves down here in El-Khârga, there was a different doctor here then, he was old and an alcoholic, and I bought morphine from him, tons of it, and so we were able to manage, the two of us, until he died and I had him flown home."

She was still looking at me with this matter-of-fact seriousness. "But I just couldn't be there, at home," she said, "even if that's where he's buried, I had to be here, this is where we were, this is where I can feel him."

I nodded while looking into her eyes. At first I'd thought she was dealing with her pain exceptionally well, that's how her eyes looked, as if she weren't afraid of it, the pain, and the sorrow, but still I wasn't so sure, she was clinging so hard to this godforsaken place.

"He's here," she said, gesturing with her hand, "I can talk to him here." So that was what she was doing when she sat there without moving, forgetting to drink. "And I have to finish the conversation before I can go home," she said.

NORTHEAST OF THE GILF EL-KEBÎR, OCTOBER 1958

Human skin differs from that of most mammals in that it is naked, since the hair covering it – with the exception of select areas – is confined to fine, scattered lanugo hairs. It varies in thickness, and in general it can be said that it is thicker on the extension side than on the flexion side.

The corium, or dermis, is densely filled with very small, finger-like projections, the papillae, which are copiously filled with blood and supplied with nerves and sense organs, the end organs of the nerves. These are present in especially large numbers on the tips of the fingers where the papillae are also arranged in regular, arcing lines that are particularly clearly visible on the fingertips.

All skin has a rich supply of blood vessels and nerves. Blood vessels reach from the subcutaneous membrane into the dermis, large trunk arteries that gradually branch out into smaller arterioles, and then a fine network of capillaries that form arching loops to supply the outermost layer and the papillae. The blood surges quickly and powerfully, filling the capillaries and then draining back into the venules and the veins. The nerves are also numerous and quite ramified and end in different ways in the outermost layers, some as small, bulbous swellings that are especially numerous in the papillae, and some as Pacinian corpuscles and Meissner's corpuscles.

The skin is the organism's protection against external effects. The epidermis plays an important role in thermoregulation and has a significant ability to resist the effects of heat, cold and chemicals; in addition, an intact epidermis is the best protection against bacteria and other contagions. Likewise, the tough epithelium and resilient connective tissue are important in guarding against impacts and blows.

If, however, the skin has been damaged, its ability to protect the body from external influences – whether in the form of bacteria or impacts or blows – is impaired, and these will then make their way in and affect the body to a greater

120

extent than they otherwise would have. In such cases frequent bathing and wrapping of the body or parts of it are recommended to attempt to reduce the amount of bacteria and protect the body with a type of artificial skin. Either partially or entirely. Materials made entirely of cotton are preferred for this, and, depending on the overall thickness of the skin and the severity of the injury, the fabric can be wound around the body in layers. Up to thirteen layers can be put on, but then the skin's function as an excretion organ is significantly impaired.

A medical evaluation must therefore assess where the source of the greatest risk comes from: from inside, from the body itself, in the form of hyperthermia; or from outside, in the form of

AC, October 23, 1958

COPENHAGEN AND NORTH ZEALAND, JULY 1952

   ❧ Clemens kept putting off his trip to Viborg. And he had spent almost every day with Anna in Copenhagen's summery heat. After the strong downpours they'd had in June, the city had been dry and hot, and they'd been swimming at Bellevue Beach and strolling through Dyrehaven Park and spending the nights at Anna's apartment. More and more of Clemens's things had wound up there. It had happened imperceptibly, as if they moved over there by themselves. First came the razor and the shaving cream, then the toothbrush and the underwear, then the socks and the shirts, and then the pants. And finally the books arrived too.

Anna was happy. She smiled and laughed and kissed him. She ran her fingers through his hair and blew into it when his scalp was sweaty. Her breath was just as warm as the air, but he didn't have the heart to say so. Instead he pulled her down onto his lap and kissed her mouth and let his thumbs slide over her eyebrows. Her eyes were calm, and she watched him almost continuously. Her eyes weren't closed or contemplative the way they had been when he had seen her at Regensen. And suddenly it dawned on him that she hadn't been playing her harmonica lately.

"You're not playing at all these days," he blurted out.

She shrugged and snuggled up against him. Right under his chin.

"I'm not?" she asked.

"No," he said, shaking his head. "What happened?"

She leaned forward and peered under the chair they were sitting on.

"To the harmonica? I don't know," she said. "It's not down here anyway."

He smiled and gazed down on her face, which was turned up toward his. Her ear was resting against his shoulder. She was looking at him.

Sometimes he would say, "Don't devour me all at once. Save a little of me

122

for tomorrow. You may just get hungry then, too."

"I've never been good at saving things," she would reply. "Whenever I got candy as a kid, I gobbled it all up in one sitting. I've never been able to save."

Clemens grinned. There were plenty of men who would have been scared of her rapacious appetite; they would have been afraid of disappearing down the throat of a woman like that.

In the middle of July, they went to the summerhouse Anna's family owned in North Zealand, north of Copenhagen. Anna's maternal grandfather had built it back in 1913. Back then it had been just a little shack with a kitchen, a living room and one bedroom, but the house had grown with the family: every time a new member was added to the family, be it a baby or a new boyfriend or girlfriend, the house produced an extra room or an addition to the kitchen or living room. And now it had grown into a large, light-grey barn of a building with a glassed-in veranda and an enormous deck made of tarred boards.

Anna's mother, Kristiane, and her mother's sister, Thora, had taken over the house when Anna's grandmother and grandfather got too old to look after it; after Anna's mother died, her share of the house had passed to Anna's father and to Anna.

The house was on the boundary between the plantation and the sand dunes, and there had always been a path through the blue lyme grass from the house down to the shore. But often there were scattered clumps of these miniature, sickle-shaped blades of grass right in the middle of the path. Sharp as paper. And when Anna was a child and only rarely wore shoes, she always walked this path with her eyes trained on the ground. All of her attention was focused on those pale green clusters. She didn't want to cut her feet. The same feet that were already stained black with oil from the beach. The big ships gliding across the horizon, way out there where the earth curved, leaked oil and driftwood. Tattered planks and shredded plastic containers. Blue sacks and drenched men's shoes without laces. Obviously the sailors walked around in dress shoes out there on those ships as they swabbed the decks with green saltwater and didn't mop up after themselves. Or maybe the British chucked them into the water. Men's shoes. First they would take the laces out and wind them tightly around their fingers, and then they would throw the shoes out to sea. The steel-toed ones sank to the bottom, but the rest bobbed along in the waves over the North Sea. Most of them washed ashore along the west coast of Denmark, but some floated all the way up through the Skagerrak and down into the Kattegat until they washed up onto the coast of North Zealand.

"Put your foot right there," said Aunt Thora in a firm voice when she came up to the house.

Anna turned around and put her foot on the table, so the sole of her foot faced up. Like a horse about to be shod. And Aunt Thora set a cotton ball over the mouth of the kerosene bottle, turned the bottle upside down and then back up again. All of it in a flash as if she never did anything else. After which, in rough, capable strokes, she rubbed the oil stains off.

"There!" she said with a nod of satisfaction. "Off you go!"

"Off I go?"

Aunt Thora sighed and pushed Anna through the door into the kitchen.

"We're eating," Aunt Thora said.

"We're eating?" Anna asked.

Thora put the kerosene bottle away in the cupboard under the kitchen sink, grabbed the pan of mettwurst and meatballs and pulled Anna outside. They were sitting on the deck, which was surrounded by briar roses, eating. Uncle Oskar and Anna's father and mother. And Josef with his kippah. Well, he already had the name, as he was always saying. And little Aksel, Josef's little brother. Aksel with the tongue. That long, wide tongue with a deep groove in the pale pink flesh. He wrapped it around the greasy chicken thigh and licked as if he thought his tongue were rough like a lion's and he could tear the flesh off in shreds. Instead the grease just ran down his lips and chin until Aunt Thora dabbed him with a napkin and ruffled his hair.

"Aksel," she said.

Never anything else. Just "Aksel."

Aksel snorted and kept eating until Thora coughed and gave him a look. He only saw it if she coughed. Then he licked his fingers. Each and every one slid meticulously in and out of his mouth.

And so now she was here again, Anna was, and this time with Clemens. And Josef. Josef had been up here for a couple of weeks already. He had probably just been sitting around indoors reading, she figured. And to judge from the way the house smelled, that really was the case. All the rooms were stuffy and unventilated, but the worst was the room where Josef slept. So even though it had been a warm summer outside, he'd just been lying around under the covers getting paler and paler.

"You could've at least aired it out a little before we got here," Anna said.

Josef raised his eyebrows pretending not to understand why she would think he would even dream of wasting his time on such things.

"But welcome to the summerhouse," he said, flinging open his arms. "I was starting to get a little eccentric up here with all this seclusion."

"Starting to?" Anna asked.

Josef looked at Clemens.

"Well, whatever can she mean?" he joked.

Josef was majoring in Scandinavian languages and literature and spent most of his money on books. He bought and bought, but mostly he read and read. He always had. When they stayed at the summerhouse as kids, he would spend days on end in bed with books. Anna read a lot too, and they usually pounced on the same books. Which is to say that whenever one of them got excited about a new novel, the other one was convinced that that specific book must be the most interesting book in the world, actually the only interesting book. At these moments no other books existed, so if Josef was lying in bed with *The Last of the Mohicans* or *The Courier of the Czar*, Anna was leaning against the doorway with her arms crossed, waiting. Even if he was only on page twenty-seven. Really the goal was just to irritate Josef enough to get him to surrender the book so she could get her hands on it. If Anna was the one lying there in bed, they would just swap roles, so now Josef would be standing there with his arms crossed and his lips pursed in irritation.

Sometimes when Josef wasn't reading he would instead walk around the plantation talking to himself while holding branches in his hands and flapping them like bird wings. If Anna found him doing this on one of her rambles through the woods, she would sneak back in a big arc to avoid him. She didn't want to see the look in his eyes when she caught him. She'd tried it one time and since then she'd succeeded in avoiding it.

"Where do you think we should sleep?" she asked Clemens. "There are four free rooms to choose from."

They went around the house opening all the doors. They had opened the windows and the scent of the sea and conifers had already started to make its way into the rooms. One room was off the living room. That was the original bedroom from 1913. And the glassed-in veranda with the small mullioned windows from a metre over the floor all the way up to the ceiling was on the other side of the living room. In the middle were the French doors out to the deck. From the glassed-in veranda they went out into the hallway that was decorated with framed children's drawings.

"Aunt Thora always framed our drawings," Anna said. "She saw them all as expressions of profound earnestness."

Clemens ran a finger along the wall just under the drawings.

"What kind of weird person is this?" he asked, pointing at a drawing of a person, or maybe a teddy bear, that was so inflated like a beach ball that it was starting to rise up into the air. The creature was trying to hang onto a tree.

Anna smiled.

"I drew that one," she said. "Is there a year on it?"

She looked at the drawing more closely, and in the lower right corner she could just make out 1942.

"So you were thirteen," Clemens said.

She nodded.

Back then her body was like a heart. It would swell up and then contract. Back then her skin sheathed her body, clean and taut. There were no blemishes. No bumps or bulges, no wrinkles or dimples.

It had started at night. She would sneak to the kitchen, to the icebox. And open the door to a world of roasted meat with crispy fat around the edges, apple cake from the day before, pâté de foie gras, cheese, sausage, and blackberry jam that she would wash down with the yogurt in the bowls on the kitchen counter. Most of it came from Anna's grandmother, who lived out in the countryside, because Anna's mother rarely cooked.

Anna ate and never got full. But her stomach would hurt. At first it would swell up like a big, hard ball, but by the next day it had already started to soften, and little by little everything softened: her thighs, buttocks, arms, and cheeks. Even her neck and hands.

Anna's mother was delighted with the icebox.

"Oh, that icebox is just the best thing!" she sighed.

"Yeah," Anna nodded, eyes downcast.

"Everything used to be so much work."

"Yeah," Anna whispered.

Anna spent every summer at the summerhouse. And when she came back the next year she was ten kilos lighter and had stopped whispering. But by the end of the summer she had another ten kilos to lose. And the same the summer after that.

Everybody scrutinized her body. It was never the same. Everyone, even Anna, had to get to know it again. It went from almost skinny to plump and full-bodied to downright fat. And back again.

Anna wanted to stop the cycle. But it was like a wave that washed back and forth between opposing shores.

"Get out of here, you fat cow!" her father said. "I can't stand to look at you."

And she went. With shame surging through her.

So she spruced herself up for him. Twisted her hair and fastened it in soft swoops with her mother's hairpins. She stole some of the perfume that was in the bathroom and the make-up, which made a sort of brown mask up to her white ears and pale neck.

He watched her with rapt attention. And Anna felt tingly and warm and almost didn't notice the nausea pent up in her body like bilge water. But Anna's mother would look even more distant than usual. Except on the days when he suddenly wanted as much as possible to do with *her*. Then she would suddenly light up and smile and skip around oddly while Anna faded into the background.

From the hallway were doors leading to four bedrooms. Josef was staying in one of them, but there were still three left. They picked one with a lopsided double bed, two cracked wicker chairs that had been painted white, and a washstand with a bowl and pitcher and a mirror over it.

Once they had set down their suitcase and bags, Clemens allowed himself to fall back onto the bed. It swayed under him as he landed with his arms out to the sides. His face was one big, contented smile, and Anne couldn't help herself. She crawled up over him and settled down astride him. Her legs and feet were bare, she was wearing only a thin summer dress, and *her* face was beaming too. Imagine being here with him! In the summerhouse. Never had this place been so wonderful, and they were both still just smiling like that when Josef burst in without even knocking, going on and on about how they could have a bonfire that night and grill steaks, and then suddenly he stopped short in the middle of a sentence as if he hadn't noticed until just then, in the middle of the twelfth sentence, what position they were lying in.

"Oh – sorry," he said smiling awkwardly and backing out of the room.

But Anna ran after him in her bare feet calling that it was a good idea, the thing about the bonfire. They should definitely take advantage of the weather. And the evenings were pretty much the nicest part of the day.

"Don't you think so too?" she asked him as he stood in the doorway on the way to the shed to get a shovel.

"I guess we shouldn't do it down on the beach, should we?" he said. "There're so many tourists down there this time of year."

Anna shook her head.

"Nah, why don't we do it next to the deck?"

He nodded.

"Then we can hear the blackbird too," she said. "I already saw one up on the chimney. Have they been singing a lot?"

"I don't know," he said.

"Well I'm sure that's because you haven't been listening, have you?" she teased, smiling at him.

Clemens had joined them now. He was standing there with his hands in the pockets of his lightweight linen trousers, leaning against the doorframe.

"Should I go find some firewood?" he asked Josef.

"Yeah, come on, I'll show you where it is," Josef said.

While they disappeared into the woodshed, Anna took the bucket to get some water. She was about to pull the full bucket out over the edge of the well when they emerged from the shed.

"Do you want me to get that for you?" Clemens asked, already making his way to her.

But she shook her head.

"She's used to it, you know. She's strong, my cousin," Josef said, clomping over to the deck on the other side of the house with the shovel in his hand.

Clemens smiled at her. He wanted her as she stood there in her bare feet struggling with the bucket. Josef turned around.

"Are you coming?" he shouted.

And Clemens followed him with an armful of birch logs.

Josef dug a little hollow so they wouldn't catch the dry grass on fire, and Clemens put a few pieces of wood into it.

"Wait a minute. I'm just going to grab some old newspapers," Josef said, heading toward the French doors.

"If you just have a knife and some matches, that's all I need," Clemens called after him.

"What the heck do you need the matches for?" Josef laughed. "I mean, I can hear from your accent that you're a real backwoods kind of guy, a real Jutlander, right?"

Clemens smiled, shaking his head and arranging the wood better.

"In fact, I'm kind of disappointed you're not going to start the fire by just rubbing some sticks together!" Josef yelled with a wink before he disappeared through the French doors.

Anna passed him in the doorway.

"As a matter of fact, Clemens is an authentic, back-to-nature Jutlander, just like your beloved poet, Frank Jæger," she said. "Clemens is like a real-life Frank Jæger. He knows all that stuff about firewood and nature and all that other stuff you're always talking about."

But Josef was already out in the kitchen.

"All that stuff that you don't actually know the first thing about," she mumbled.

Clemens got the fire going and, once the flames had given way to glowing coals and they'd long since tossed potatoes in the fire, Anna brought out steaks on a platter. They were glistening with marinade and she had a bottle of Chianti in her other hand. Josef was behind her with glasses and plates and utensils and a grill they could put the steaks on.

Clemens was squatting next to the fire, poking the coals and nudging the potatoes a little with a stick. His pant legs had slid up to just below his knees, and he was barefoot. Anna put the platter of meat and the bottle of wine in the grass.

"Isn't it wonderful here?" she asked, inhaling the scent of pine needles, grass, and wood smoke.

"Yes," Clemens said. "And it's so quiet here. Especially coming from Copenhagen."

Anna nodded.

All they could hear was the blackbird up on the chimney, the fire crackling, and some children playing somewhere on the dunes.

Clemens sat down in the grass next to the fire with the glass of wine Anna had given him. He felt so peaceful here. And drunk. Not from the wine, he'd only had a few sips. But from the smells and the light over the sea, and from Anna and Josef, and from the house. There was something unfinished here, about them and the house, and it did him good.

His family's home in Asmildkloster had been finished in a different way: furnished with fancy heirlooms, heavy mahogany bureaus and cabinets, books stacked neatly on the shelves, in alphabetical order. There weren't many, mostly magazines about agriculture and forestry and reclaiming moorland and that kind of thing, but what there was, was very tidy and organized. And there had been dinner parties with attorneys and doctors and whatever Viborg – fine provincial city that it was – could otherwise offer in the way of educated men.

His mother had tried hard to fit in. She had done her best. Actually, she fit in so well that she had almost disappeared, he thought. Small and thin and bashful. Plus he could tell that there was something different about *her* mother, his grandmother from the little west coast town of Vejers. She had been crazy, pure and simple, there was no sugarcoating it, he had understood this from his father. But they had managed to hide her away. Clemens also saw that his own mother had inherited some of the insanity. In a very diluted form. And, generally speaking, Thorkild had managed to keep what was left in check. She had become a straight line, his mother. All her intricacies and fluctuations had been flattened out. Clemens smiled and thought of Halvorsen. If Halvorsen had set her to music the way she was when she was younger, surely she would have sounded like a theremin or a musical saw, sliding from one undulation to another, a series of notes that clearly had a harmonic basis but were always becoming inverted and discordant. Now she was a middle A. An unremarkable concert pitch.

Clemens had never been afraid of the distortion, the discord. He'd encountered it with Ane, and especially in the "Anna Blossom" poem she had read to him. And he had been fascinated. And now he had found Anna. It was as if he had come home. Home to Anna Blossom. He saw it in the grey house, and he saw it in Josef and his family. He didn't see it in himself. Not that it *couldn't* be there. The question was sooner being able to see *what* it was to begin with.

But it was like there was room for him here, there was a hole that had just been sitting there waiting for him to come and fill it. It sealed up around him and he slid blithely into this world.

NORTHEAST OF THE GILF EL-KEBÎR, NOVEMBER 1958

Leo is sick. He started coughing a few days ago. I was somewhat surprised wondering if it was really possible for anyone to catch a cold in this heat. But now it seems more like the flu. He's lying in his tent with a terrible headache, and his temperature is quite high. This morning it was quite high, up around 40°.

Anna is looking after him and making sure he has water. She's always very attentive at making sure that everyone has enough water, but now she's extra dedicated to it. Seeing that Leo gets enough. And that we all wash our hands.

But the expedition needs Anna other places than in that tent. She's too wrapped up in caring for Leo. I've told her that, but she gets mad and says that she isn't sure it's the flu. And even though I've tried to explain to her that Leo is strong and that the fever will go away on its own, she keeps checking on him all the time.

CC, latitude 24° north, longitude 27° east. November 3, 1958

NORTHEAST OF THE GILF EL-KEBÎR, NOVEMBER 1958

ॐ Sahara means "abandoned" or "deserted."

Everything disappears in the desert. The sand, which is as fine and light as flour, wafts away and covers everything. Skeletons, rocks, and villages. And the sounds disappear. Muted by the sand. And people disappear, too.

If you walk just twenty metres away from your companions, over a dune, you may risk not finding your way back. You've disappeared.

Little by little, the Sahara filled Clemens.

NORTHEAST OF THE GILF EL-KEBÎR, NOVEMBER 1958

ॐ Clemens was sitting at the table in the shade under the awning. From the tent. He was sitting at the table with one hand in front of him. On top of his notebook. That was lying on the map, which fluttered now and then. He was going to write. Work. He was going to write in his notebook.

He'd taken his shirt off and was looking down at his own chest. There was hair. In the hair there were drops. Slowly. They emerged incredibly slowly like little bubbles on his skin. Or permeated through it from the inside. And then they grew. They grew until they were big enough to be called drops. And then they slid through the hairs. Occasionally they had to change course because they had to move around the hairs. One hair could constitute an obstacle. He was going to write. In his book. He had a pen in his hand. But he didn't know how to lift his hand. He had to lift his hand to write. But it was still lying there, on top of the book. It was holding the pen. His fingers were holding the pen. There were a few hairs on the back of his hand. Ten or fifteen if anyone were to count them. But he didn't. He tried to lift his hand so he could get something out of it, the hand. Work.

Then he got up. He stood next to the table. With one hand on the tabletop. Or sooner the fingers of the one hand. His fingertips were touching the tabletop right next to his notebook.

132

NORTHEST OF THE GILF EL-KEBÎR, NOVEMBER 1958

I'm worried about Leo. This is the second week he's been sick now and his fever is still quite high. He's listless and altered and has been suffering from constipation.

I'm afraid Leo has typhus.

He may have contracted Salmonella typhi in the four days he was gone. That was almost four weeks ago and that would match the pathological picture. If I'm right, the bacteria have already penetrated his intestinal mucosa to the underlying tissue and have spread from there into his blood stream. And presumably, it has already permeated into the immune tissue of the small intestine, so I can expect diarrhea in the next day or two.

I have, of course, started to medicate him. I'm treating him with antibiotics and hope with all my heart that they can beat back the bacteria so he doesn't develop peritonitis.

I've quarantined him so I'm the only one who goes in to him and I've asked Sayeed to be extra careful with the hygiene. Of course everyone should wash their hands all the time.

I'm tired. And I can tell that Clemens is too. He sits at his table a lot. It doesn't seem as if the work is proceeding quite as quickly for him as it has before.

I'm really very tired. And sometimes I feel a little out of it. Like I'm not quite myself. Then I try to write. When I feel like that. Actually I'm not exactly sure what I write, because I never read it afterwards.

It feels good to write, but it doesn't feel good to read what I've written.

AC, November 15, 1958

NORTHEAST OF THE GILF EL-KEBÎR, NOVEMBER 1958

᠍ Clemens sat at the table in the shade under the tent's awning. He'd been writing in his book. The day before, for example, he'd written in his book. Anna was also writing. She was sitting on the other side of the fire, writing. Well, it wasn't burning now. But when it was burning. When it was burning, she didn't sit on the other side of the fire. She sat on the other side of the fire pit when the fire wasn't burning. Because it was daytime. Anna wrote during the day. When she wrote. Anna didn't write at night. At night she moaned.

Clemens wasn't sleeping at night. Couldn't sleep during the day either. Clemens sat at his table. Sometimes he wrote. The day before, for example, he'd written. He was working. Clemens wanted to work. But he was tired. He had to rest a little at the table.

ॐ Finally I've had some news. Hamad down at the Provincial Office called me, some information came in from the search party, they'd met two Brits on a motorcycle somewhere out in the desert, I didn't quite catch where, and some time about two weeks ago they had come across two Danes who matched the descriptions of my mother and father.

So they were alive, two weeks ago at any rate.

It was a relief to hear that. If they were alive two weeks ago, why shouldn't they be alive now? I mean, they know what they're doing. In terms of the desert, at least.

I'm taking this awfully fast, I know that, but last night she was suddenly just standing there, Helga, asking if she could sleep here, she was just standing there outside my door asking if she could sleep with me. Mette can be very direct, but it's more in a practical way, she would never just stand there and ask if she could sleep with me, and she certainly wouldn't do that if she didn't know me.

There's nothing practical or efficient about Helga, and it's like she's completely devoid of conventions and formalities. They just don't interest her at all.

Helga is one hundred percent Helga. She's uncommonly serious and matter-of-fact, actually she doesn't laugh at all, but she doesn't come across as morose, she just looks at me with these eyes that have this tranquility in them. I would pay a fortune to feel that kind of tranquility, even though obviously I'm quite a bit older than her so I really ought to be the one with eyes like that, although actually I guess I have no idea how old she is, I totally forgot to ask her that, we just sort of skipped over all the formalities. I mean, she didn't beat about the bush, she just up and asked me if I loved my wife!

It's funny, sitting here, I just have to keep shaking my head, it's like I have a hard time believing what's going on around me, and in me, I can't believe I said I didn't love Mette.

I don't love Mette. I do not love her. She isn't the one I love. Evidently, it's that simple to say.

I'm in love with Helga, that's an easy thing to say, I know, I'm a thirty-five-year-old man, I ought to know that you can't just go around claiming that kind of thing about a woman you hardly even know, and especially not if you're married and have been for years. But so many things seem different here, nothing works the way you would expect.

It's her earnestness. When I picture her, I see those eyes, they're enormous, and I think they seem much bigger in my mind than they actually are, I mean she blinks now and then, it's not like they just stare, those eyes, and yet they're completely tranquil, whether she's talking about grieving for her dead husband, asking me if I love my wife, or asking if she can sleep with me.

So, is she completely free of all the baggage the rest of us carry around, the stuff that makes us squirm? Is it that she has no shame, suffers no self-reproach? Is she clueless about the way she and other people are supposed to act? Does she not feel people's eyes on her the way so many of the rest of us do? Can she experience sorrow and pain without letting it eat her up inside? I don't know her well enough to know the answers. But I think so.

So, of course, I let her in, and of course I said she could sleep with me, it made me feel warm to see her standing there, she always stands with her weight evenly distributed on both feet, of course she does.

I offered her a seat, but she didn't respond at all, she walked over to the window and started looking out. I do have a fantastic window, it's the best thing about the room, it's an ornate, beautifully carved Islamic-style window, and I can see the minaret from here and hear the muezzin.

"So, have you been remembering to stay hydrated?" I asked, and she turned to look at me and nodded. "Good," I said. "That's very important." "Yes," she said, "I know that. I'm remembering to drink enough now." "Good," I said again and then I asked if she was hungry, if I should see if I could scrounge us up some food. "That would be lovely," she said, but she would be happy to walk over and get some, too, walk over and get some, yes, she would never use any other word, she wouldn't say "run out" or "pop out and get some," no, she walks. "I can picture you as a nomad," I said. "I can see you walking at a leisurely pace alongside a camel, all the way across the Sahara, from east to west, the same tempo all the way across." She looked as if she were considering whether she could see herself that way too, then she said, "Yes, maybe you're right." And then I went and got some food, and when I came back, she was leaning over the table with all the photographs of my parents, and the stacks of their notes and journals, and my computer.

She picked up one of the photographs, it was from the summer of 1952, thank God all the pictures are dated, there's a little year on them, and sometimes the month is there too, on the back, that's been a great help to me in my reconstruction work. The photo she was holding was taken at the summerhouse in North Zealand, my mother is sitting in the grass looking straight at the camera, my father is behind her, squatting, so you can see his knees on either side of her, his lips are at her throat, and his eyes are probably closed, you can't quite make it out, Josef is walking around behind them with a broomstick balancing on his chin, his thin arms stretched out to the side, while he tries to keep the broomstick upright.

"Is she pretty, your mother?" Helga asked, turning the picture a little. I was surprised that she was talking about my mother; people, especially women, usually focus on my father. I shook my head. "Pretty? No, she's not," I said. "No," Helga agreed, "she isn't pretty, but what a face she has!" "Yes," I said, "that's her all right." Helga nodded. "How can eyes be so present and so absent at the same time?" I moved over to her and took hold of the corner of the picture and tilted it toward me a little so I could see it better, "Yes," I said, "How can they?" We didn't know.

That night she lay with her back tucked in against me and her head resting on the inside of my upper arm, with my hand I caressed her forehead and her hair, I didn't say anything, she did the talking.

I wanted her – don't get me wrong, I really wanted her, but she wasn't present, and I would never have dreamt of trying to make her be present, not because I'm some magnanimous gentleman at heart, but with Helga everything has its own tempo, and as a rule it's a serene one, almost drawn out, and trying to change that is just completely out of the question. There are some things you wouldn't even consider messing with.

But I was forced to rotate a little so she wouldn't notice that I was lying there with a hard-on.

Suddenly she got quiet and I cautiously lifted my head so I could see her face. She was asleep. So I tried to pull my arm back toward me, because it was starting to fall asleep in the somewhat awkward position I'd been lying in for such a long time, but she grabbed onto it, and I had to give up and see if I could fall asleep with the blood prickling in my veins.

When I woke up the next morning, she was lying there watching me, and all of the sudden I was so happy to look into that face that I grabbed hold of it and kissed her.

"I want you," she said, in the same matter-of-fact way that she'd asked last night if she could sleep here.

COPENHAGEN AND NORTH ZEALAND, APRIL 1953

۵ Anna opened the window. It was the first day of spring. The sun was shining, and she could hear birds singing from over by Sankt Petri Church. She'd bought daffodils this morning and now they were standing on the table being yellow.

Gray's Anatomy was lying in front of her along with various pages of lecture notes, but she was pouring over Werner Spalteholz's *Hand Atlas of Human Anatomy*. Anna would put her hand over the parts she was supposed to have memorized, look straight at the bouquet of daffodils and mouth the words with her lips. There wasn't much time left before the final exam, but that didn't matter today. It was spring and the light was streaming in over her. Actually it was bugging her a little, the light. It was hurting her eyes, and she should have shut the curtains, but that would be like turning her back on the spring and summer, Anna thought, squinting.

Then she heard footsteps on the stairs. It was Clemens. She was never wrong, she knew exactly what his footsteps sounded like. He always bounded up the stairs. Two or three steps at a time. She took a deep breath and smoothed her hair.

The door swung open, and there he stood, out of breath with daffodils and a big smile. He saw the daffodils on the table and his smile faded slightly. Then he shrugged and walked over to her and set the flowers down in front of her.

"It's the first day of spring," he said, leaning his torso out the window.

"Can you feel it, Anna?" he asked, turning to face her. "It's spring now!"

She smiled up at him.

"I was just sitting here enjoying it," she said, leaning back in her chair.

"Is spring the only reason you're so happy?" she asked.

"Come on!" he said, reaching for her. Then right after that he said, "No, wait, stay there!"

"What is it?"

"I got permission to go on Lindholt's expedition!" He practically shouted it.

"You did what?" Anna asked, feeling how the blood sank throughout her body.

"I'm going on an expedition!" he said, standing in the middle of the room, at attention like a soldier. "I'm going to Morocco! To the Atlas Mountains!"

Anna stood up.

"You're going to go to the Atlas Mountains?"

He nodded emphatically and looked pretty much as happy as she ever remembered seeing him.

"No!"

She practically screamed it, and Clemens jumped.

"Anna!" he said, grabbing her shoulders.

"No!" she said again, shaking her head. "You're not leaving."

"What are you talking about?" he asked.

"You have to stay here," she said, starting to cry. "Here with me."

"Yes, but darling," he said, pulling her in to him. "I am coming home again. It's only for a month."

She pushed herself free from his embrace.

"You have to stay here! You can't leave."

"OK, but Anna can't you see how important this is to me? I'll be able to use this for my dissertation, and that will make it easier for me to get a position at a university later on."

She sighed.

"It's what I want," he said quietly, but earnestly.

"And what about me? Aren't I important? Don't you want me?" she asked. And now her voice was defiant.

His body deflated a little.

"Of course," he said, sighing at the same time, so the words flowed out on a wave of air.

"That makes it sound like I'm some kind of a burden," she said.

Clemens took a deep breath.

"You think I'm a burden!" she screamed. "And you're happy about the thought of getting away from me!"

Her voice was quivering, and a fiery redness spread over her neck and face. Clemens looked at the floor. But suddenly she fell silent and turned her back to him. She walked over to the dresser by the door. She pulled a drawer out and then slammed it back in again.

"I'm scared!" She yelled it in a voice that was much deeper than normal. "I'm scared of what will happen if you leave."

"Anna!"

Clemens went over to her and put his hand on her shoulder. She turned around.

"I'm afraid of what I'll do if you leave," she said.

After Clemens left, Anna went up to the summerhouse in North Zealand with all her books so she could study for her final exam there.

She got off the train in Hillerød and had to run to catch the red streetcar that would take her through Grib Forest. The trees were black and the plants in between them still yellow, but Anna could see that spring was here. It must be the light that was different. And a single skylark hovering over a clearing in the woods.

Anna got off at the tiny stop between the big pine trees. There wasn't even a shelter here. Just the platform and the pines with their tops sweeping against the sky. It was a different world up there where the birds and the wind and the green needles were. But down among the tree trunks you could hardly feel the wind. You could only hear it soughing and sighing, and now and then a cloud would pass over a hole between the tops of two trees.

She left the road and took a shortcut through the plantation. The path was compacted dirt, and it wound in and out through the spruce and oak trees. It was starting to get dark so Anna sped up. She wanted to get to the house before it got dark.

It was cold in the little kitchen when she let herself in, and there was that distinctive odour of must in all the rooms. Everything seemed strange, and Anna felt a sense of uneasiness like a sinking feeling in her stomach. She sat down in front of the woodstove in the living room and arranged a couple of logs with kindling and newspaper around them. The flames shot up the instant she put the match to it, but the kindling didn't catch and the flames went out as quickly as they'd started, leaving porous flakes of newspaper behind.

But the fire took the second time and the wood was fully ablaze. Anna shut the door, opened the flue and looked around the living room. Soon it would be safe to be here. The furniture would start to look like itself again, look like it did when they were all here together and the rooms were warm.

Once she got the fire going in the living room, she went to the kitchen and opened the little hatch on the woodstove. She pushed the ash into the back corner and then put in wood and newspaper. The woodstove had always been easier to light. This chimney drew better and the fire started quickly.

After that she went to the well with the bucket they kept hanging in the kitchen on a peg. She set it down and flung open the lid to the well. Then she turned the winch and lowered the other bucket, the one that always hung here in the dark, down until she could see that it was touching the water. The trick was to get it to hit the surface of the water sideways so the water would flow into it as she let it glide from the one side of the curved stone wall to the other. Then she turned the winch in the opposite direction and the bucket, filled to overflowing, would right itself and rise back up until she could reach it and, using both hands, hoist it out over the edge of the well and pour the ice cold water into the bucket from the kitchen. She carried it back to the peg where it hung with the ladle floating on its surface like a little boat.

It was warmer in the house when she came back in, and she took off her coat and hung it in the cramped porch. It'll be good to be here after all, she thought as she tried to ignore the sinking feeling in her stomach. Only a month. In a month he would be home again, Clemens. Four weeks. Twenty-nine days. And she could stay here as long as she wanted. The whole month if she was having a good time. And she'd be able to get a huge amount done without him here bothering her. She would be able to get through all the reading she needed to do before her exam. It would be good.

After two days Anna had succeeded in reading three whole pages and the furniture hadn't started to look like itself yet. But the place had warmed up.

It was important for her to keep the fire going. The coals must not go out under any circumstances, and preferably she would add new wood before it got to the coals stage. It was best if there were flames all the time. So it was a matter of paying close attention to the wood burning stove and especially now when there weren't many real logs left, just boards which burned astonishingly fast. So she had to adjust the length of her walks along the beach and through the sand dunes to match the amount of time the boards took to turn into coals. And at night she set her alarm clock to wake her up every three hours so she could put new wood on. The cold mustn't be allowed to creep in.

Not that it was cold any more. It was April after all, well, the beginning of April anyway, and spring hadn't really taken hold yet. It was just lying there lurking. But still. It was April.

After another three days had passed, Anna heard voices outside the house. Loud voices and laughter, so she hid in a corner so she couldn't be seen from the windows.

There was a knock on the door and someone called her name.

"Anna! Hello, Anna!"

And now she could hear who it was. It was Josef and Aksel. So she ran to the door and opened it.

"What are you guys doing here?" she asked.

"Well, we found out that you were up here all by yourself so we figured we would come keep you company," Josef said with a big smile.

"I'm pretty busy," she said. "I'm studying for my exam."

"Yeah, yeah," Aksel said. "We're going to study too."

Josef held out a paper bag and said, "Beer. We brought beer."

Anna shook her head. And Josef tousled her hair.

"Now don't be boring, Anna. That's not like you!"

She smiled at him.

"It's nice that you guys are here," she said. "Did you bring food too?"

"Food? What do we need food for? We have this," Aksel said, nodding at the beer.

Josef went out onto the porch to take off his duffel coat.

"Actually you should keep that on. Since you're here, you guys can make yourselves useful," Anna called from the kitchen. "Wouldn't you like to bring in some firewood?"

She ran into the living room for the basket.

"Here," she said.

They headed over to the woodshed. Josef in front with the basket in one hand.

"Hey, Aksel!" Anna yelled.

She'd opened the top half of the door.

"Bring some for the oven too!"

Aksel raised his hand and Anna shut the door and went back to the kitchen. She hurried over to the little mirror that hung next to the plate rack. It was her eyebrows; they were so thick and they got messed up so often. She licked her finger and used it to slick them down. Now if only she had lipstick. Well, this would have to do.

When Aksel and Josef came back in, Josef set the basket next to the wood stove in the living room and Aksel stacked his logs on the floor in front of the stove in the kitchen. Then they hung up their jackets on the porch. Their wool sweaters were soon to follow.

"You've got it nice and warm in here," Josef said, taking his sweater off and tossing it on the sofa.

There wasn't much food in the house, but there were eggs, so Anna made fried eggs with rye bread and herring, and they found a bottle of schnapps in the back of the kitchen cupboard.

"I bet your dad hid it there," Aksel said.

Anna didn't say anything; she was frying eggs, and it didn't take long before they were spattering in the pan and the water for the tea had started simmering in the pot next to it.

144 ◊ KAREN FASTRUP

"Ah, how cozy," Aksel said, settling in.

And now Anna could feel it. It was cozy here, and it was nice that they were here, that there were voices in the house and the clatter of pans and porcelain.

Josef set some beers on the table.

"No, Josef!" she cried. "Put a tablecloth down first."

"It doesn't matter," he said.

But she was already there with the tablecloth, unfolding it underneath his hand from which the beers were hanging like the teats on a cow.

"There!" she said, smiling at him.

"Since when did you care about stuff like that?" Aksel teased as he set out the plates and glasses.

"I'm going to get married soon," Anna said. "So I have to learn all this stuff. You know, try to domesticate myself a little."

Josef snickered and ran his fingers through her hair again.

"Domesticate? You?"

He shook his head, and she tried to swat him.

"Cut it out now, Josef," she said. "You've always been after me."

"Someone has to be after you," he said. "Otherwise who knows what you'd get up to next."

"Humph," she said.

Aksel grinned.

"Josef, do you remember that time she forgot it was Christmas and didn't get here until after everyone was already done opening their presents?"

Anna gave him a pretend slap. "You guys talk as though you'd always been models of behaviour!"

"Well we were," Josef said, smoothing down his hair. "*Models* of behaviour!"

She shook her head. "You guys were always a couple of uncivilized beasts! How was that you used to eat, Aksel? You used to lick the meat into your mouth until the drool was dripping off your chin! You ate like a wild animal!"

"Certainly not," he said. "That couldn't have been me."

"Um, yes," she said. "It certainly *could* have been you."

"Oh, right. That *was* me, wasn't it?" He opened his eyes wide, and slinked toward her with his arms out. "Well, that's because I'm a wild animal!" he said, pulling her head back.

"Aksel!" she shouted. "Cut it out!"

His face brushed by hers so that his nose almost grazed her cheek.

"I'm wild!" he whispered.

Josef pulled him away and pushed him down into one of the chairs at the table.

"All right you fool!" he said. "Now eat!"

"Am I really related to you guys?" Anna asked, smoothing out her hair and straightening her cardigan before sitting down and dividing the white mass with the yellow eyes into three sunny-side-up eggs and easing them onto the plates.

At the same time, Josef poured schnapps into the glasses.

"Hey, Anna," he said after contemplating his plate for a moment. "I thought you said something about how you were trying to become a little more domestic?"

"Yes?" she asked, nodding.

He gave a smile to Aksel.

"Well, now, at a traditional Danish meal, you do know that the fried egg doesn't come first, right?"

Anna jumped up, covering her mouth with her hand.

"Oh my God! The herring!" she said, reaching for their plates to slide the eggs back into the pan.

But Josef grabbed her hand.

"Aw, come on! It doesn't matter," he said. "We'll just have a shot of schnapps with our eggs *and* a second one with the herring."

Anna sighed, shaking her head.

"I guess I'm never going to get the hang of this," she said.

"Just as well," Josef said. "I mean it's not like you're just going to be some kind of housewife. You're going to be a doctor."

He reached for the schnapps bottle, held it up to the light to see how much was left, and poured another round into the glasses.

They ate a lot and for a long time, and Anna had to slice more rye bread, but when she got full, long before the other two, she leaned back in her chair and took a good look at them, these cousins of hers that were as permanent a fixture here in the house as the table they were sitting around, as the chairs and the striped cushions that Aunt Thora had sewn just after the war. The features on Aksel's face were still soft like on a big baby, and his cheeks were smooth as if he couldn't grow a beard even though he was twenty-three. It was different with Josef. Beneath his youthful face with its unwrinkled skin and bright eyes he already bore the face he would have when he got old, with the thin lips and the cleft chin, the bushy eyebrows and the crooked nose with the fine veins. At times it seemed grotesque to see him running around with this face. Loud and full of laughter. Not restless and unfocused, but fierce and without any particular consideration for anything besides his need to keep moving.

In the evening they pulled the chairs over to the wood stove. There was still some beer left, and they drank what there was. They also found a bit of vermouth next to the jars of rose hip marmalade in the glass-front cabinet in the kitchen.

"So, have you guys read any of Frank Jæger's poetry yet?" Josef asked.

Aksel shook his head.

"No," Anna said.

Josef kept one of Jæger's first two volumes with him at all times, *Virtuous Poems* and *Morning's Trumpet*. Discovering Jæger had been like finding his own, true self. Finally he was able to see who he was: a healthy, bona fide man. Finally he had found a mirror that didn't distort or blur, that reflected him crisply and precisely. That was what he was like, that was him, Josef. It gave him a sense of confidence and complacency he had never had as a child or teenager. Finally it was all right to be Josef, yes – actually, it was amazing. Josef Jæger, as his friends from school started calling him, cultivated his raw, untamed naturalness to such an extent that he would often either neglect or offend other people. Not because he meant bad, far from it, just because after so many years of trying to see anything besides fog when he looked in the mirror he had finally seen himself. And the reflection was so big and so dazzling that all other reflections, both his own and other people's, faded away into the darkness behind this reflection of Josef Jæger.

He jumped up out of his chair and ran to his room, returning an instant later waving his book around.

"Listen to this," he said, flipping through it.

Anna pulled her legs up under her, and Aksel looked at her.

"If only the world were a thousand times bigger,

rougher, cruder than it is," he read while gesticulating with his free left hand.

"If only its creatures sat like a dense,
gooey cake, if individuals were
copiously frosted with sins and mistakes –
and also bigger than shipwrecks
and with long, uncut hair."

Josef's face was ablaze and his eyes glittering.

"And listen to this," he said, flipping ahead.

"No more!" Aksel said.

"Yes, listen to this," Josef said and read:

"An easy-access vagina
clenches shut in despair…"

He ran his hand through his hair and then continued:

"Her thighs move in spasms
inside the smooth condom of her dress.
And I play my greasy con

man role to the core:
without paying I sneak
along the walls out into the rainy streets."

"Isn't that amazing!" he exclaimed, slamming the book shut. "So raw. So true!"

"Sure," Aksel said, sitting up in his chair. "That's amazing, but we're going to need to have some more to drink."

"Oh, no," Anna said. "No more!"

Josef, a little deflated and annoyed because his brother didn't want to talk about Frank Jæger, suddenly snapped out of it and jumped up.

"Yes," he said. "Damn it, we'll have some more!"

And then they went around, Aksel and Josef, opening cupboards and pulling out drawers. But the only thing they found was a decanter with a slosh of schnapps and a stalk of bog myrtle in it.

"Well, we'll have to make do with that," Josef grumbled as they came back into the living room again.

"Don't you think even you have had about enough?" Anna asked.

She was sitting on her knees in front of the wood stove, putting in more wood.

"Good grief, Anna, we need to have a little fun," Aksel said, plopping down onto a chair.

Josef went to sit down too and, although his aim was a little off, he managed to correct it in time so he hit the seat of the chair without seeming too clumsy.

Anna shut the door on the stove and stood up. She noticed that Josef's eyes were following her. He'd been watching her. His eyes were glassy from the beer. And from her, she thought. She followed him with her eyes. His eyes misted over a little, but he kept watching her. She looked over at Aksel. He wasn't as drunk, but he was watching her too, and aside from the fact that his eyes weren't misting anywhere near as much as Josef's, the look was the same. She sat down. They desired her. Both of them. She had no doubt about it. And when you got right down to it, they always had.

Especially Josef used to roughhouse with her. When they were little, it had been irritating to be suddenly knocked down or pushed into a chair. But when Josef started going through puberty and grew that Adam's apple that bobbed up and down in his throat, there was something else. He kept knocking her over when they were out on the dunes, but he didn't tumble around with her quite the same way as before. Now he lingered, lying on top of her longer and making his body heavy. So heavy that she almost couldn't breathe and had to yell at him to move. And it so happened that her father saw that and he got such a strange look on his face, his look made it seem like what he was seeing was disgusting, and then he pulled Josef up and shoved him down the side of the dune. On days like that it was always a long time before Josef showed up again, and Aunt Thora would walk around shouting his name and asking if anyone had seen her Josef, and then Anna would look at her father, and the lines around his mouth would get harder and his eyes seemed smaller than usual. Something dreadful had happened. That much Anna was able to understand.

Josef got up to go out and pee, and as he passed behind Anna, he put his hand on the back of her neck. Heat flashed down through her. She wanted to just lean back and let the heavy breath that was dammed up in her chest flow out. It was the beer, she had had too much to drink. But she couldn't let Aksel see. It was one thing for Josef to realize what the situation was, but Aksel sitting over there, little Aksel, he shouldn't see it. She tried to clear her eyes before she looked over at him. She wanted to see if he'd noticed anything. He had, that was obvious, because his eyes were resting even more heavily on her than before.

Josef came back in again; he wobbled a little as he maneuvered around the dining table. Anna could sense him behind her. He just stood there, and she didn't know what was going to happen until she felt his hand again. This time it slid all the way up over the back of her head. In under her hair with his fingers spread apart so he was holding her whole head in his hand. She couldn't hold it any longer and the sound slipped out of her mouth. The breath. She had gone over to the other side.

Yet she could still see her father's face in front of her. Those dour lips and eyes. Something dreadful was happening. She realized that, Anna did.

Aksel sat on the floor in front of her and pulled her pants off while Josef, who was still standing behind her, kissed her throat and unbuttoned her cardigan so he could hold her breasts. She raised herself up a little so Aksel could get the pants off her, and she was so wet and open that she could hardly feel his finger sliding in and out of her. Then he licked her, and her own tongue had never felt so long and so agile as it did now, clinging to Josef's.

Josef pushed Aksel away, unbuckled his belt, and took Anna as she sat there, leaning back in the chair with her thighs out over the armrests. He had a hold of her hips with a grip that cut into her flesh, and he hammered into her with the same fierceness with which he usually moved around out there, on the dunes.

Anna moaned a little and looked up at Aksel. His eyes were on fire, and now he really looked wild, she thought. He clutched at his belt and started undoing it.

Then, she screamed. So loudly it startled them. And she pushed Josef away and grabbed her underwear and pants and ran out of the house. She raced through the dunes and down to the water. They wouldn't follow her, she knew that. Surely they were arguing up there in the house now. Yelling at each other. She plunged out into the water. It was cold, but the wind had died down, so there were only gentle swells. She spread her thighs and washed herself, her hands scrubbing and scrubbing at her crotch.

Anna walked along the beach toward Gilleleje. Her pants were clinging to her wet legs, and she was freezing. There was a full moon, and not a cloud in the sky. The dunes and the plantation behind them, which she caught a glimpse of every now and then behind the valleys between the dunes, were bathed in an unnatural, blue light. Everything was visible, and everything was casting shadows. Long and crisp.

She got colder and colder and started jogging as much as she could, given the heavy sand and her legs that were getting stiffer and stiffer in the nighttime cold. But finally she reached the station in Gilleleje where she huddled on one of the red-painted benches on the platform. The first train of the morning wouldn't come for a couple of hours and it was getting colder. It's coldest just before sunrise, she knew that, but at least she was dry now. She tried to relax her body to get it to stop shivering and her teeth to stop chattering, but she could only do it for brief spells.

Anna cried and called out for Clemens who probably wasn't even thinking about her as he walked around down there in Morocco among those men he admired and respected. It was probably a relief for him not to have to deal with her. And here she sat in the dark, colder than she could remember ever having been before. And where should she go? The keys to her apartment on Larslejsstræde were back at the summerhouse with her clothes and books, and she didn't want to stand there without a coat, begging the landlord to let her in. And she couldn't turn to her father either.

On the train from Hillerød to Copenhagen she realized that she could go to Aunt Thora's on Holsteinsgade. That's what she would do. Take the streetcar from Central Station in Copenhagen and get off at the Triangle, and then just hurry down Holsteinsgade. There won't be many people out on the street this early in the morning either.

Aunt Thora opened the door in her bathrobe with an expression of disbelief on her face.

"Anna!" she exclaimed. "You're here?"

The apartment on Holsteinsgade was one of those big Copenhagen apartments that was frozen in time the instant it was built. And amid the 1890s architecture was strewn Aunt Thora's clutter: socks, frayed canvases, sketch paper, chipped vases, paintbrushes, empty tubes of paint, scarves, painted canvases, books, carpets filled with holes and half-eaten hunks of rye bread.

Anna's mother Kristiane had never been quite like this. Although that's certainly the direction she would have headed in if she hadn't met Anna's father, who was rather organized and always knew where everything was. Anna's father probably fell in love with her mother because she contained this chaos, because scarves fluttered from her hair like they did from Aunt Thora's. Because she would get all wrapped up in nothing. She could stand in front of the mirror for half an hour at a time and do nothing besides twist and twist the scarf around her hair. Slowly and laboriously, but without really seeing what she was doing. It was just the motion and the feeling of the material against her fingers and the feeling of the scarf tightening around her head. Here I go, she thought and smiled the smile that always drained away before it had properly settled on her face. Not because she didn't mean it, not because she was actually sad. But simply because she wasn't in the same place as the people or the thing she was smiling at. She was just swishing past for those brief seconds it took to prepare for a smile, then she slipped away again.

All of that was what he'd fallen in love with, Anna's father. And a man could go and fall for a woman like that, but he couldn't be married to one. She couldn't keep house, and he couldn't show her off to his colleagues at Funch & Son, the successful engineering firm out by the barracks on Prinsessegade where he worked. He had tried once or twice, and they had looked at her with an expression of desire and contempt that he had previously noticed that men adopted when they looked at her. Because she was pretty. There was no doubt about that. With her curly, red hair and her jewelry. But it was as though she was from somewhere outside of time, her style was completely out of date and her attire was eccentric. And then she would hardly ever answer when someone asked her something. Maybe she would start, but the sentence would fade away in the middle and then they would stand there, his colleagues, waiting for more. But it never came. She just looked at them while bending her neck in crazy motions as if she were doing gymnastics.

She never was able to fulfill the role of housewife. But they were married, and a divorce was out of the question. He had to go and get mixed up with her and her sister, and her sister's sons, and Oskar, her sister's weird husband, a professor who was almost as absent-minded as Anna's mother. But in a different way. He got things done. He read and studied and wrote newspaper articles that were published in *Politiken* and he was always working on something. But he also never talked. So they could sit across from each other, those two, Anna's mother and Oskar, and just stare. Now and then Oskar would look up from his books and glance at Anna's mother who was sitting across from him and staring past him into the distance. Occasionally he would be lucky enough to catch her attention and they would nod slightly to each other before she slipped away again and he lost himself in the letters on the pages in front of him.

But Anna's mother died young. Actually it should never have happened because it was just a simple cold, but she died all the same. And it seemed completely natural. It was as if she were just repeating the journey she always took. Only this time she didn't snap out of it, but stayed out there in the lifeless void where all her sentences and smiles had wound up.

Anna was fifteen when her mother died, and after that she alternated, living part of the time with her father and part of the time with Aunt Thora. Aside from the summer months, when they were all at the summerhouse.

Thora was messy and chaotic. Even more so than Anna's mother had been. But at the same time she was far more composed and better able to function. She understood what was going on around her, and she was pretty much never in doubt about what she should do about it. She was in charge in that family, however much good that did with Aksel and Josef who hated having anyone be in charge of them. "Why are they so wild?" Anna asked one time when she was little. "Oh," Aunt Thora answered flinging out her arms, "because it's so messy here." Anna nodded, looking around. That made sense, she thought.

And now she was standing there with no coat on early one April morning, chilled to the bone.

"Well, come in, come in, Anna!" Aunt Thora said, pulling her into the dark hallway with the glossy lacquered floorboards.

One time Anna hadn't been able to help herself and had lain down on her stomach and stuck out her tongue to feel that smoothness. Running her fingers over it hadn't been enough. She'd done that before, but they were even smoother. There wasn't any roughness against her fingers. Well, then, maybe her tongue – which was much more sensitive – wouldn't feel any irregularities, a little chip or a scratch? Or was that the limit to the smoothness? The tongue? It wasn't. There still weren't any irregularities and Anna wanted to eat the boards. It was too titillating that it just kept going and going, all that smoothness.

Thora offered Anna a seat on the bench in the kitchen. She made her some coffee and buttered French bread. The coffee smelled good and the bread was soft under the cheese, so Anna ate and drank until there wasn't any left.

"Well, let's hear it," Thora said.

Because she knew something was up. She felt sort of the same way about Anna as she had always felt about her sister: she was her own person, maybe not quite as much as Kristiane was, but as a result she was more fragile. Since her sister had almost not been a part of this world, she had avoided most of the worries it entailed, but Anna was more present. Although she seemed stuck out in the margins, as though she had never really made it any further than the edge of the world, Thora thought. Kristiane had given birth to her out there on the other side, and since then Anna had spent most of her energy trying to crawl into the world, to where the rest of the people were. The people who always knew when to say things like "thank you," "you're welcome," and "don't mention it." But she never got any farther than the edge. Still, that was close enough to be messed up in it, in the world, and thus to be exposed to its worries and concerns.

"Well, let's hear it," Thora repeated. "What happened?"

She looked concerned and Anna didn't have the heart to mention Aksel and Josef. And what had actually happened? How had it started? She shook her head.

"I'm so tired," she said, laying her head down on the table.

"Where's your coat?"

Anna sighed.

"It's all up at the summerhouse."

Thora stiffened and nodded. She knew full well that her boys were up there, but she had not known that Anna had been there too.

"Are Josef and Aksel still up there?" she asked. Her voice was clipped. Not cold and accusatory. Just resolved.

"Yes," Anna said.

Thora took a deep breath. "Did something happen between you guys?" she asked. This time her voice sounded tense. She spoke lightly and quickly.

Anna shook her head. As best she could, since her head was resting on her arms on the table.

"But I kind of need my stuff," she said.

"Yes," Aunt Thora said. "You'll kind of need your stuff."

Anna nodded.

"We'll have to get Josef and Aksel to bring them back," Thora said.

"Yes, if they're coming back soon."

"They are. I'll call the grocer up there and get his delivery boy to give them a message: they have to come back today."

Later that afternoon Aksel and Josef were standing on Holsteinsgade. Thora opened the door and let them in. She didn't say anything, just studied their faces to see if she could figure out what had happened up at the summerhouse.

Aksel bent his head down and Josef looked right past her. But when Anna came into the living room from the bedroom where she'd been resting, he walked right over to her. Thora didn't say anything, she didn't want to get mixed up in it, she just hoped that her son could find a decent way out of the whole thing. Whatever had happened.

Josef stood in front of Anna. She was leaning in the doorway, staring down at the floor. Josef's eyes were also downcast. He was standing in front of her, but he couldn't keep his arms still. He was fidgeting with his hands and every now and then he would hit the outside of his thighs with them. Then he looked at her.

"It was too much, huh?" he said.

Anna nodded, but kept looking at the floor. She couldn't look him in the eyes, because she couldn't figure out why it had been too much and who was actually responsible.

He nodded too, but didn't say anything else. Until he suddenly said, "Sorry…. From Aksel too."

She looked up at him. He was ashamed, that was obvious. But his eyes were also warm.

Then he held out his arms.

"Here," he said, as if he wanted to give her a hug.

Anna dropped her arms and went over to him. She didn't take hold of him. Just stood there looking up.

Then he said, "Little Anna." As if he were talking to the Anna she had once been. Before he gotten his Adam's apple. And now she went into his arms and let him hold her. The worst thing that could happen now was that he would push her over or onto a piece of furniture. And that was the kind of thing you could live with.

I couldn't sleep last night so I sat down at the desk and flipped through my mother's book. She seems to be going over the edge here. The edge where she came from.

She's lying on the table with her legs resting against the iron. They're spread. Her thighs. He sees that as he stands there with the pack. And his spine is way too short so the pack seems to be squashing his body down toward the floor. His eyes are like gashes in his face. But little by little he is able to make things out in the darkness in there and he can just make out her labia, which are persistently unfolding and unfurling, a profusion of blood-filled petals. He bends forward and riffles through them. One by one he pulls them from one side to the other. His fingers become wet and slippery. There's nectar flowing over the petals.

A sound pushes its way in from somewhere outside. He stands back up and licks his fingers clean. It's the wind. It tugs at him. And his tongue glides down over the throbbing petals and in between them. It wasn't the wind that made the sound. It was the soul rushing out between the lips. Someone is breathing.

He bends forward again. The nectar is flowing down over the inner thighs in long, sticky threads. With his tongue he follows the trail. Back and in. He drinks. Like a cat he laps up the liquid.

AC, November 23, 1958

154

EL-KHÂRGA, DECEMBER 1996

) There's something I don't understand.

Last night I extricated myself from Helga's arms and went to sit at the desk, the light was bluish, and the air seemed open, and I had a sense of space, both in the room I was sitting in and in my lungs, space to take deep breaths, as I sat leaning back in my chair and looking out through the carved window, looking over at the minaret.

I don't have a printer with me, but can you believe it, even here in El-Khârga there's an Internet café where I can send e-mail and print out the pages I've written, and as time goes by there's getting to be quite a few, they're lying here in front of me along with my mother's book and my father's notebook and the various loose pages I've had sent to me too.

I've never known them as well as I do now, my parents, I think I've gotten a sense of why they were the way they were, not that I have exhaustive explanations, and I'm not a big believer in the idea that you can get to the core of a person and analyze everything. That seems reductionist to me, there's always going to be something left over. But my impressions have gotten clearer.

Did I mention this already? I may be wrong, of course. A lot of things may have happened differently from how I've portrayed them, that's obviously a condition of engaging in deductive reasoning. Which is not to say that it's possible that everything I've written is pure nonsense, pure conjecture, not at all, I truly believe that I've made every effort to go about this openly and conscientiously, but I suppose the truth doesn't just come in one shape or size, at any rate not in cases like this. It's not like the truth is going to light up and start beeping when you happen upon it. The truth doesn't call attention to itself like that, it's out there somewhere, and now and then I'm sure I bump

155

against it, or maybe it's not out there in just one place. Maybe it's in lots of places. Maybe it's not a river, but a whole watershed of creeks and streams and tributaries and estuaries.

But there's still something I don't understand.

Not that you can just list the events in someone's life and say that because my mother was unfaithful to my father there has been this wound between them ever since. The wound may have started long before that, their skin may have been broken long before they met each other, but at the same time they've loved each other, I've never had any doubt about that, and they've desired each other, I've never had any doubt about that either, they've been chafing at each others wounds and keeping them open. Not as a conscious act. But as an inevitable process. Like weathering or erosion.

Natural processes have no conscience. Neither good nor bad.

But there's still something I don't understand.

I don't understand why my father never seemed like a jilted man, an innocent man who'd been betrayed. I don't understand why mostly he was the one who seemed burdened, tormented by remorse.

My letter to Mette is in the computer, I wrote her that I want a divorce, I feel for her, of course I do, and I've been tormented by my guilty conscience, but now I mostly feel relief, I'm free, I'm alive.

NORTHEAST OF THE GILF EL-KEBÎR, DECEMBER 1958

A hand breaks the light. A drop hangs from each fingertip. The drops get longer and longer until the surface tension breaks and a bead of water releases its hold on the finger and glides through the air before being absorbed into the cracked earth. When five drops have disappeared this way, another one and then one more land on the edge of a puckered scar in the earth's crust. They come from the arm. The drops. From the shoulder actually. They trace long, shimmering paths down along the outstretched arm, welling up under the fingertips. The hand from the other arm has scooped up water and allows it to drip down over the shoulder of this arm. A few drops hit so high on the shoulder that they roll the other way. For a while they follow the lower edge of the clavicle until they trace an arc down the centre of the chest. Wet, wet rose petals, the song goes. We moisten our rose petals. Engine noise. There's engine noise coming from somewhere out in the desert. The voice is interrupted by engine noise. But then the noise ceases. The noise from a motorcycle. As the sound of the motorcycle ceases, the voice is counting rose petals. The drops between her breasts slide the other way. Back up over the clavicle and down along the neck. All the way down to the jawbone, just next to the ear. Now the body lies down. The face is covered with dust, and the lips are cracked. The back of the head pushes back and forth on the crust of the earth in the noise from the engine that's coming closer again and then envelops the entire body. The knees are bent and the feet are pushing the body forward and backward as both hands are engulfed in the moist folds of her vulva. Everything is engine noise until it goes quiet again and only the crinkling of the sand in the wind can be heard. The body lies motionless and the man by the motorcycle pulls his goggles away from his eyes, where they leave two conspicuous white marks on the dark, dusty skin. He pushes them up onto his forehead. He

AC, December 13, 1958

157

SMÅLAND, SWEDEN, JULY 1956

≈ The sound of a bumblebee made Anna look up. It buzzed over the grass like a chubby marble and settled in one of the sweet pea blossoms that was climbing the house behind her. She set the book on the table, it was *Sinners in Summertime,* stretched her bare legs in front of her and inhaled the scent of the grass and flowers and forest floor that surrounded her as she sat here outside Uncle Oskar's red, ramshackle cottage in Småland.

Since Clemens had gone into the woods early that morning, she'd found an old table and a couple of chairs in a corner of the woodshed and had lugged them all out to a sun-warmed corner of the yard. The grass was tall and the ground uneven, so she'd had to find rocks to put under the table legs to get the table to stand somewhat level. Then she'd had hardboiled some eggs and made coffee, sliced bread and put the cheese on a floral plate that was horribly chipped, to be sure, but still so nice that she was enchanted with it and stood there for a long time admiring it and turning it this way and that before setting the cheese on a blue flower in the middle of it. In a drawer in the bedroom she had found an old lace tablecloth, full of holes, sure, like everything else, but pretty and summery, and before she spread it over the table she wrapped it around her waist like a skirt. She stood in front of the mirror and cocked her head. Then she unwound it again and went back into the garden, wearing just her underwear and an undershirt. It was already sweltering and the air was stagnant over the meadow by the yard.

She set the table and sat down, enjoying the look of the food and the fancy plate under the cheese until she leapt up, scanned the edge of the woods for Clemens, who was nowhere to be seen, and ran into the kitchen for a vase and then darted out into the garden and snapped off a few pea blossoms and stuck them down into the cold water.

She'd certainly set a lovely table, she thought sinking back into the chair. But she actually wanted to dress herself up a little for Clemens. So she went into the house again, put lipstick on, just a little, you didn't need too much out here in the woods in Sweden, and found a little blue scarf that she tied around her head with a knot at the nape of her neck under the hair. The blue colour went very well with her dark hair, she thought, and she suddenly became aware of the lightness. The lightness in the air, in the scent of flowers and grass, the lightness in the sound of the swallows that were swooping around in the birch trees in precise arcs, the lightness in the buttery-yellow Brimstone butterfly that fluttered by, the lightness in herself.

They'd made love that morning. Clemens had woken her early. His breathing had been heavy and his face serious, and she'd pressed herself against him and enjoyed the feeling in her own languorous morning body that went soft for him in a flash.

It had been a long time since they'd made love. She'd graduated and started her residency at Fredriksberg Hospital. Everything was easier. Everything was actually working out for her. Her exams went fine, and she felt like she fit in well at the hospital. She could talk about everyday stuff with her colleagues. She would even laugh and kid around with them when they were sitting in the break room, and she didn't have any trouble saying the right things at the right times. She actually felt like one of the other people, like someone living in the middle of the world on an equal footing with everyone else.

But when she came home in the evenings she was tired. Her body was heavy, not like it had been this morning when they made love, but heavy in a clumsy way, as if every muscle was a hard little nodule. As if the only thing holding her up were these nodules lying on top of each other, making her movements stiff.

Clemens looked at her. Not affectionately or amorously like he had before. But as if he were scrutinizing her. When she saw herself in his eyes, she saw a woman she didn't know. She could see that he was trying to get to know her again. This woman who *functioned*. Far better than ever before. He could go away if he had to, without all that fuss, and she would go to work everyday and be a good doctor. No doubt about it, and he was proud of her. But he missed his Anna Blossom. Because he had sometimes *had* her. She would go away for long periods of time when she'd sit with her hair over her face and play or just sit there staring into space, but then she might suddenly snap out of it, out of herself, because that's where she was, inside herself. Now she was nowhere, it occurred to him, just gone. And now she only came to him very rarely, and he missed his own fragile Anna with the harmonica, Anna who suddenly looked like she wanted to gobble him up with a ferocity he hadn't thought women could possess. But she functioned poorly with other people, his Anna Blossom, that wasn't hard for him to see. She was nervous and knew that she didn't know the conventions. All of these things that people say and do with the greatest matter-of-factness. This way of navigating the rules and the standard turns of phrase that most people had mastered, allowing them to navigate through a safe, familiar landscape – for Anna it meant desperately meandering through unknown and perilous rocky formations. And so, time after time, she shrank back, reluctant to go out there.

What was amazing, Clemens realized, was that, now that she had ventured out, she was getting to know the paths, she was starting to feel safe out there. But she couldn't get out of it again. This landscape. There wasn't any other Anna besides the one who meandered around trying to make the perilous paths safe and familiar, trying to flatten out the landscape into a terrain that was even and easily surveyed.

But she did seem to be doing better, he thought. So he resigned himself to the situation and devoted himself to his books and kept working. And things were moving along at a furious pace with his career. He was thirty-one and had finished his dissertation a long time ago and been hired as a researcher in the department. He was accomplished and well liked and had been chosen to be the youngest full member on the expedition to the Qattâra Depression in northwestern Egypt earlier in the year. It had been a rough trip, but then they had been in one of the most dangerous places in northern Africa and, despite his youth, he had gradually taken over the leadership of the expedition in practical terms because the official leader had turned out not to possess the qualities a leader needed under the mentally taxing conditions that an expedition to such a remote region necessarily involved.

Clemens, on the other hand, had proven to be the perfect expedition leader. He was calm and authoritative, able to see the big picture, and always reliable; he didn't despair when some unexpected complication came up, he didn't get depressed or irritable, he didn't let the other team members' pettiness or mood swings get to him. He remained serious and composed whenever there was any sort of problem. He was strong, Clemens was. That's how he appeared anyway. And that was all that mattered in that context.

And there he was, emerging from the woods over there on the other side of the meadow. He flung his arm up in the air and waved at her.

"Anna!" he hollered.

She stood up.

"I saw moose droppings!"

She shook her head.

"Lots of them. And they were fresh."

She sat down and waited for him. The coffee was still hot under the tea cozy, but the eggs had gotten cold.

He sat down across from her, and she looked at him expectantly.

"This looks great," he said.

She nodded, beaming.

He smiled to himself and reached for the coffee. Sometimes she was like a child. She made things look nice and admired them and couldn't wait to show him everything, and then when he looked at it and appreciated her efforts, she never hid her pleasure. He liked that side of her, he felt a tenderness for it, and on the whole he could sense how his love for her had grown or had regained its old strength in the two days that they'd been here. It was as if she were starting to come back to him. Of course there weren't any other people here for her to relate to or anything else for her to do.

When he'd missed the old Anna the most he'd asked where she was and said that he wanted his Anna back. Then she'd turned her head away a bit so as to avoid his eyes and told him to leave her be. She hadn't yelled or been mad, more than that she had sounded a tiny bit scared. As if she were afraid he would ruin her hard-won ability to function. "I don't want to be like my mother," she'd said, and so he'd let it drop. She had her reasons, he thought.

But now she was happy and beaming under the blue scarf she had wound around her hair.

"You look wonderful, Anna," he said.

And she smiled and passed him the bread and let him see the fancy plate the cheese was on.

"Isn't it nice?" she asked, lifting up the cheese just as he was about to cut a slice.

"Hey," she said, letting go of it again so it toppled down onto the plate, which was just about to topple off the edge of the table.

"It is beautiful here," Clemens said a little later.

Anna nodded.

"So how did your family wind up with so many houses anyway?"

Anna shrugged. "They're all a bunch of dilapidated old shacks anyway," she said. "Crooked and leaning."

"Well then they're in great company," he said, grinning.

She shook her head and pulled her legs under her. Then she suddenly stretched one of her legs over the table. "I really do have very nice legs," she said.

Clemens nodded, pushing her foot away a little. It was on the verge of knocking over his coffee cup.

"I like the ankles best," she said.

"The ankles?" he asked, his mouth full of food.

"The ankles are the most important part of a woman's leg. If they're fat, the rest of the leg looks shapeless."

"Is that so?" he asked, leaning back.

"Yes, it is," she said.

After they washed the dishes they found an old bike that was covered in cobwebs. Clemens pulled it out of the shed and brushed it a bit with one hand while Anna ran inside to get a rag. There was only one bike, so she had to sit on the back for the two kilometres down to the lake; when they got there, Clemens's undershirt was wet in a triangle over his back.

There weren't any designated swimming beaches on the lake, but there were several big, flat rocks they could jump in from, and after they stripped off their clothes Clemens jumped in and Anna saw how magnificent it looked as his white body slid down into the ochre-coloured, ferruginous lake water. After a moment he popped up again further out and called to her.

"Is it cold?" she yelled.

"Yes!" he said.

"Well," she mumbled, sitting down so she could stick one foot in and inch her way in.

"This is painful to watch, Anna," he yelled from out there, doing the crawl toward her so that the water, with the sun shining through it, washed over his torso.

But before he reached her, she'd made it all the way in, splashing and screaming.

"Oh, it's freezing!" she yelled.

"Start moving," he advised.

And so they swam out. On one side the lakeshore was encircled by tall spruce trees that jutted into the sky, on the other were a couple of fields that had just been harvested where row after row of hay was lying out to dry all the way down to the lakeshore. A couple of cranes were walking around cautiously, and with those long tufting ornamental feathers down over their tails they resembled elderly ladies with their hands on their backs focusing all their attention on the ground so they wouldn't step on a spot that was slippery or uneven.

When Anna and Clemens got to the middle of the lake, they stopped swimming and treaded water so they could appreciate the quiet. There wasn't any noise besides the spruce trees, which occasionally rustled softly over by the shore, and then a couple of Canada geese that took flight further out on the lake, churning up the water behind them.

"Things are going so well here," Anna said, drawing in close to Clemens.

He nodded.

"Couldn't we live here?" she asked.

"Do you want to live here?" he asked.

She nodded and brushed the hair away from her face.

"And have children," she said.

He smiled.

"What about when I have to travel?"

"Then I'll go along."

"You'll go along?"

She nodded.

"I'm definitely coming next time no matter what."

He looked at her.

"Out into the desert?"

She nodded.

"That's in a year and a half," he said.

"I'm coming."

He shook his head and started swimming back toward shore.

"Come on!" he called out to her.

As they clambered onto the rocks the water slid off them, leaving small drops on their skin. Clemens lay down on the warm stone; Anna sat cross-legged, tipped her head forward and started drying her hair with the towel.

She watched him as she did it.

"One of the things I like about Sweden is that the countryside is idyllic and raw at the same time," she said, nodding over toward the fields on the other side.

"There are fertile fields and farms over there and over here are trees that could just as easily have been further north. In the mountains."

She looked around.

"Isn't that so?" she asked.

"Hmm," he said.

He was lying on his back with his hands behind his head.

"The countryside isn't so plain here," she said.

She set the towel down and pulled her knees up under her chin. With the fingers of one hand, she dabbled in the surface of the water.

᠅ We've been back in Denmark for two months, my mother and father and Helga and I, and they *did* clean up the house out there in Lyngby. The rugs have been hung up again or are stacked in the big piles my mother stores them in, and my father's rock collection has been put away.

But I've lost track of *my* story, or at least pushed it aside, and now of all times when I was so close to being done.

I went down to see Josef yesterday, in his used bookstore. Yes, he sells used books and his shop is located three stories underground in a cellar full of books and he's doing great. "Tore!" he exclaimed as I stepped in, or down, into his world of dust and letters, "Tore, welcome home!" because I hadn't seen him since I'd gotten back and then he mussed his hair, he's always doing that, and it's starting to get a little thin, and a bit crazier, actually, because his hair got coarser after it turned white, it had been quite dark, and now he has a beard. Now? Now... that makes it sound like he just grew the beard, he didn't, he's had that since the early seventies when the two of us, he and I, used to trot around wearing buttons that said "Nuclear Power? No Thanks!" and those light blue ones that said "Renewable Energy" and whatever all the other ones were, all the slogans for the various causes we marched in support of, and we used to march all the time, Josef and I, there was nuclear energy and then there was something about women, and we went to Germany one time, without work visas, but yesterday he was sitting there in his cellar, reading.

"Come in, come in!" he called out, slipping out from his little nook behind the counter where he sits and reads and keeps track of his inventory, and contemplates which estate sales he'll go to and which ones he'll skip. "Come in, Tore! So great to see you again." "Same here, Josef," I said and told him that I had a new girlfriend. "Wonderful," he said, closing his eyes, "wonderful," and then he picked up a book and waved it around, "Is that the book you're reading?" "No, I just finished it," he said, "I just finished it. What a piece of shit, Tore, the damn author ran out of steam, I don't know," he said, "but he didn't finish it properly. You know," he said, "you read and read, and a whole story unfolds, and then what happens in the last chapter? Everything falls apart. As if he didn't stick around to find out what happened, the guy, the author. So then what happens? The last chapter is bad?" I nodded, but Josef shook his head, "No," he said, "if only you got off that easily, with a disappointment. But no, you get betrayed: the people, the lives, that you were part of, become false. Everything you believed becomes untrustworthy."

And actually I think he's right, Josef is. The last piece of a story interferes with everything that preceded it, like a flashback it reaches back through time and changes everything, and you can change someone's understanding of a life in much the same way. A person does a thing, and that thing makes you see him in a whole new light.

Maybe that's what I'm afraid of. In a way I suppose I've ended up sitting here with my parents' lives in my hands, I'm the one who decides how their story ends. Not that there are a lot of possible endings, there's only one that's correct, there was just one thing that happened down there in Bîr el-Shaq in December 1958.

And I can certainly make room for it.

Maybe it's my dislike of endings that has made me put off finishing my story. Maybe it's the divorce from Mette, or the separation, we're still just separated, divorces take time, the government sure sees to that.

I let Mette keep everything, I mean it's not like I brought anything with me when I moved in with her. In the meantime, of course, I've acquired some books and a computer and some clothes, and I took those with me, that's all I brought with me when I moved in with Helga, too. That's the second time in my life I stepped into a woman's apartment almost empty-handed, but there was a big difference: whereas Mette had almost everything, Helga had almost nothing.

But maybe it's just my discomfort with what happened in December 1958 that's made me put off the ending. Suddenly discovering that everything is different from how I'd pictured it so far.

❧ It says, *Coca- ola*. The "C" is missing. From the sign that squeaks on its rusty chains, hanging there under the eaves on Harun's house. There are two Jeeps next to the building.

I drove out here with Helga and Dhahab Abaza, who's our chauffeur and guide, I do not have any of the qualifications required for someone to even just move around alone out here in the desert, and I had to fork over a lot of American dollars to get him to drive all the way out here. To Bîr el-Shaq.

The house has been here since some time in the forties, it belongs to the Province, which is responsible for making sure that the cistern is tended so that people travelling by on the caravan route toward 'Ain Doua can get water.

Now you can also buy Coca-Cola and cigarettes and Bounty and potato chips, and back behind it, by the little mud brick annex, there are drums of high-octane gas that someone drove all the way out here from Abu Simbel way back when UNESCO sent a bunch of scientists to save Egypt's cultural heritage from being flooded by the Nile when they were building the big Aswan dam.

On the way out here, I asked Dhahab Abaza to stop for a bit, because I was so damn scared, I'm not quite sure what I thought we'd find, maybe that's exactly why I was scared, because I didn't know what to expect, I mean there was no way to know what had happened to my parents. I still don't know what happened at Bîr el-Shaq in December 1958, or if anything did happen, anything significant, I mean, because obviously *something* happens all the time. But it is striking in any case that all of their notes come to a stop at the camp northeast of the Gilf el-Kebîr in December 1958 just before they went to Bîr el-Shaq, and from there on to El-Khârga and Cairo. I don't have anything after the Gilf el-Kebîr.

And now we're standing here. In a heat so intense you almost want to scream, that's how claustrophobic it is. But thank God Helga came. She just got out of our four-by-four, she left her door hanging open, and now she's looking around, she isn't wearing sunglasses so she's shading her eyes with her hand. I suppose I'm sort of both in the car and out of the car, I've opened my door, standing with one leg in the sand and the other on the running board, but then Helga says "come here" and starts walking over to the house with the *Coca- ola* sign.

An old man appears in the doorway, and I'm guessing it's Harun. His nose has a sharp bend in it about a finger's width below the bridge so it never really manages to stick out from his face, it's sort of clinging to it, he looks different from how I'd imagined. We walk over to him, and he starts saying all kinds of things in Arabic that we can't understand, we only understand all the politeness phrases, we don't understand the rest, neither Helga nor I, and then he starts talking about Coca-Cola, *that* we understand, but we shake our heads and say no thank you, or *I* shake my head and then I say my parents' names, "Anna and Clemens," I say, I say it two times, and then he nods and opens his mouth slightly, and after nodding once he says "Anna and Clemens" too, and then I'm the one nodding and I say, "Here? Are they here? Anna and Clemens?" I say it all in English and for good measure, I repeat, "Here? Are they here?" And then he nods vigorously and smiles and says, "Yes."

We scramble up onto the top of a seif, and Helga says she wants to eat the sand, "It's all the grooves," she says. "Dig in!" I say, and when we get all the way to the top, we see them.

My mother is wearing a long, white galabeya and her hair is hanging down against her back in a braid, "She has white hair?" Helga asks, "I thought her hair would be brown." "What in the world were you thinking?" I say, "She's sixty-seven years old!" "Of course," Helga says, "I totally forgot they weren't young. I guess I'd started thinking we were coming out here to find a couple who was the same age as us. Or at least the same age as you," and then she smiles, shaking her head.

My mother and father are walking side by side, they're walking slowly, very, very slowly, we can see, and every now and then they stop walking altogether, they stop and turn to face each other and talk, they're talking calmly I can see, also my mother, because when she gesticulates she does it very slowly, she forms the words in the air with her hands. My father's are in his pockets.

We sit down, Helga and I, we're sitting on top of a yellow seif dune and looking out over the desert, we're looking at two white figures in a yellow desert, two people who then turn around and head toward us. I find myself feeling something intense, I'm not totally sure what, but it's something that tugs on my diaphragm, and I feel the urge to cry, I don't, but I feel awful.

Helga is sitting next to me, cross-legged, staring straight ahead, looking down at the two figures. "I hope," I say to Helga as I see them walking there side by side in their white clothing, my father is also wearing white, after all that's what's most comfortable in this heat, "I hope," I say, "that I still have my parents. Together." "Yeah," Helga says, "I hope that for you," and I say, "I hope it for myself but even more for them, because now they're not just my parents anymore, now they're two human beings that I know very, very well and that I… I care so much about them, Helga," I say. "My dad, too, even though he's so different from me, and he certainly is different, Helga," I say. "Yes," she says and nods, but she doesn't take her eyes off them, "Yes he is, very different." She's read what I've written, otherwise obviously she wouldn't be able to say something like that.

My mother and father are standing at the foot of our seif looking up at us. "My father's been crying, Helga, my father's been crying!" I say, "I can tell, and you know, I've never ever seen him cry before," but his face is calm, he glances calmly and seriously up at me, and so does my mother, although not seriously, she smiles and yells "Tore!" and I stand up and so does Helga and then she starts walking down the seif. Her feet leave deep tracks in the sand, which comes alive and trickles down into the sides of the craters left by her sandals, and I follow her, but she's already way ahead of me.

Helga holds out her hand first to my father and then to my mother, they seem somewhat surprised, and I can hear Helga introducing herself and saying that she's my girlfriend, and I bite my lip and stop for a second, but then my father starts smiling as he yells to me that it's damn well about time, "About time?" I say, starting downwards again, and then I say, "Yeah," but then I stop speaking, because now Helga is talking.

She's standing just in front of them and saying a whole bunch of stuff, her backbone as straight as ever and one arm hanging down at her side, the other shielding her eyes, it's the sunglasses, I told her she should remember them, and now she isn't saying anything, now my mother is talking and Helga is looking at her, and then she turns to my father and says something to him, and then he says something, he says a lot, I can see, he talks for a long time, and then he puts one hand up to his eyes, not because of the sun, that's behind him, he rubs both eyes and then he glances up at me and calls out my name and I go down to them.

My mother puts her hand on the back of my father's head and he tilts his head back a little, into her hand, and then she says we'll all end up getting heat stroke if we stay out here much longer and then my father asks if he can't treat us to a *Coca- ola* at Harun's place.

It feels good to enter the cool, stone house, and Harun grins and nods at Helga and me while he says a bunch of stuff to my dad that I don't understand, and my dad says something back, and we sit down, and my mother studies Helga, rather intently, I might add, and Helga is fully aware of it, she notices, I can tell, but it doesn't matter, from time to time she looks my mother in the eye, and then she asks what happened here at Harun's cistern in December 1958, and that startles me, because I mean I've been wondering, thinking quite a bit about, actually, how I was going to ask, what my approach would be, and then she just asks, "What happened?" she asks. "What happened at Bîr el-Shaq in December, 1958?"

BÎR EL-SHAQ, DECEMBER 1958

꙳ A man was standing in the salt lake outside a little desert village in northwestern Chad. The desert wasn't reddish yellow here. It was greyish white. And the same for the houses. Even the man's bare legs took on a greyish hue as he stood there in the middle of the salt lake. The greyness settled like a membrane over his black skin.

He was bending over forward in the warm brine, scraping the bottom with a wide-blade hoe. Once the salt was disturbed it would sink and he would fish it off the bottom and move big clumps of it into an iron pan. After that he mixed it with soil and packed it into molds made out of hollowed trunks of palm trees lined with leather. Carefully he would turn out the molds and the salt cones would slide out into the sun where he laid them out to dry.

When there were enough salt cones, the caravan would move on. Four men and twenty-one camels loaded with salt, with millet the men could eat along the way, and with enough fodder to feed the camels for the entire trip out and back. For a total of twenty-one-hundred kilometres.

A caravan only stops at night. Otherwise it doesn't. There isn't time to stop. The men knew how long it would take to reach the next well, Bîr el-Shaq. And the water rations were calculated so they would last just long enough. If the caravan moved sixty kilometres a day.

Black men with their faces and bodies wrapped in cloth. They were the Tuareg, or the Blacks, as the Arabs called the people from Chad and Niger. Silent, with bodies that swayed softly with their camels. Now and then the men would hop down and walk. Kilometre after kilometre through the sand, which glowed under their feet. But after a few hours they would pull the camels' heads down and hop up onto their necks. The camels would bellow

170

and the men would crawl further up onto their backs. All this as the caravan glided along.

In a goatskin sack which one of the men wore hanging over his shoulder was a porridge of water and millet. It had been cooked the previous night and was now stiff and dry. But while the men and the animals wandered away, the man poured water in and shook the sack so the porridge softened, after which it was divvied up into bowls for the men.

The caravan slid through the desert like a snake. When it got dark and there wasn't anything left to see other than the whites of the men's eyes, the caravan leader would navigate by the stars. The temperature fell, and the men wrapped carpets around their black bodies as they walked.

The caravan didn't stop until it had been moving for eighteen hours. The men unloaded the camels, fed them, lit a campfire and made food. But there was no time for sleep until two in the morning. For three hours. Before the salt caravan moved on the next morning toward the cistern.

The expedition had been planned to last for eight months, and by then Leo was very sick. It had now been two and a half weeks since he'd shown the first symptoms, and he still had a high fever and was alternating between shivering and lying drenched in sweat that trickled out of his skin and ran down over it.

One moment he would be hallucinating, and his body and face would be agitated and tense; the next moment he would collapse in exhaustion, seeming far away in a fever-induced stupor. He had also developed diarrhea.

But Anna could tell that the antibiotics were keeping the disease at bay. They hadn't eradicated the bacteria yet, but they had prevented peritonitis.

Anna had insisted several times that they had to leave. That they had to get Leo to a hospital. But Clemens thought he could hold out until the expedition was over. They only had a few days left anyway. And, after all, he did have the best doctor tending to him and looking after him. And they had medicine too.

So no one insisted any more. Just as the desert muffles all sound, it had also muffled their will. So Anna tended to Leo. She tried to pour water between his lips, which cracked more and more. And he wasn't able to swallow the pills, so she crushed them between two spoons and mixed them with a couple of drops of water so she could let the solution slide into his dry mouth. She sat with his head in her lap. She stroked his hair dampening the cloth in the water she kept next to her and wiping his face before placing it on his forehead. Then she would start again at the beginning. She also tried to pour some of Sayeed's soup between his lips. Drop by drop. And otherwise she rocked him.

All as Clemens watched.

But a few days later, the expedition was over and they were on their way to El-Khârga. The bumpy Jeep ride was so hard on Leo that they were forced to spend the night in the annex at Harun's cistern.

It was cool inside and Anna and Peter spread out rugs on the dirt floor and laid Leo on top of them. Anna sat with her back against the wall so she could hold Leo's head in her lap while resting her back. She had her doctor's bag next to her.

"Do you think he'll survive?" Peter asked, subdued.

He was standing there leaning against the mud brick wall.

Anna ran her fingers along Leo's jaw. His face was yellow and drawn. She nodded.

"Yes," she said. "We have the right medication. So he'll make it."

Peter sighed.

"But I can't give him enough fluids," she said. "I don't have an IV."

Peter squatted in front of her and looked down at Leo.

"But he'll make it," she said. "The fever will break."

Meanwhile Clemens was sitting outside. He felt tired and worn out. He'd been having trouble sleeping for a long time. The emptiness that had gradually taken root in him since October as everything else had slipped out of him, was slowly being replaced by a painful desperation. The emptiness hadn't been pleasant. But there had been something numbing about it.

Now it was as if all the feelings and sensations he had pent up in there were starting to trickle out. They were growing like stalactites in his body's empty caverns. They were still small and hard, but something was starting to happen. He sensed it, sitting there under the eaves. There was a scratching and a rasping inside him as if the stalactites were cutting into his abdominal cavity. Shredding him from the inside out.

He hid his face in his hands. The skin of his face was warm, and he felt dizzy. After a while he lowered his hands and examined them closely. But they were empty. There wasn't anything stuck to them.

Then he jumped up. His body was on fire and it felt so strong, the way it only ever did otherwise right before an orgasm.

"Anna!" he yelled.

That night the caravan from Chad came. The first thing Clemens noticed was the bellowing of the camels. They were agitated because they could smell the water. But it still took some time before he was able to see anything through the dense darkness. Then they came into view in the light around the fire – the men and the camels. And Clemens and Sayeed and Harun stood up.

After watering their animals and hobbling their forelegs, the men sat down by the fire and Harun offered them some of the *margannana* that he and Clemens and Sayeed were already smoking. Two of the men started playing the small drums they'd brought with them. The rhythms were thumping and penetrating, and the men started singing. Plaintive tones, songs of the greatest woman of them all, the one they loved and feared: the desert.

Clemens had fallen asleep by the fire with the men from the caravan. But when they started stirring and getting the camels ready, he woke up and, still disoriented with sleep and *margannana*, he went into the annex. Peter was sleeping in Harun's house, so it was just Anna and Leo. Anna was asleep, half lying and half sitting up against the wall. She was breathing heavily. But Leo's breaths were shallow. And he was drenched in sweat. The room smelled stuffy and sickly sweet. Of sweat and skin, oily with the miasmas that a sick body gives off.

Clemens sat down next to Anna. Right up against her but without touching her. He sat that way for a long time, maybe twenty minutes, before he opened her medical bag, took out the boxes of antibiotics and stuffed them into his pocket.

When Anna woke up at dawn, chilled to the bone, her muscles stiff from the awkward position she'd slept in, she reached for the mug of water sitting beside her. She dipped a finger into it and let is slide around Leo's lips before she tried pouring water directly from the mug into his mouth. Even though he seemed far away and heavy, his lips tried to mold themselves to the mug, and his tongue moved in his dry mouth.

Anna opened her doctor's bag to give Leo his pills. They weren't there.

She got up and went outside into the clear morning air. The sun was nudging a streak of gold up over the horizon ahead of it, but otherwise everything was still grey. With a rug wrapped around her shoulders, she went all the way out.

The fire had burned down, and Clemens and the Tuareg caravan were gone.

Leo died two days later. Without the medicine, he developed peritonitis and his diarrhea turned black with blood. He didn't come out of his feverish fog and there wasn't anything Anna could do besides wash his face and dip pieces of the cotton cloth in water and let them glide over his lips until he closed his mouth around them and started suckling the water out of the cloth.

Harun smeared black and red ointments containing extracts of the adenium desert rose and harmal seed capsules over his face and chest. And when the rays of the setting sun would shine in through the door of the annex, they fell on Leo and made his blackish-red skin gleam.

Anna let Harun do it, because there was nothing else she could do. She knew that they weren't going to able to get Leo to the hospital in El-Khârga, so he was either going to die a strenuous death in the Jeep as they rattled through the desert or he could lie very peacefully in Harun's annex.

After Leo died, Harun carried him out to the cistern where he lay him on a bed of dried palm frawns. Anna and Peter stood beside him.

Leo was Harun's now.

And once Harun had conscientiously arranged the dead body on the bier, he started hauling up water and pouring it into the basin he'd placed next to the body. When the basin was full, he washed Leo. He formed a ladle with his right hand and lowered it down into the water. Then he lifted his hand and moved it over the dead body. Individual drops trickled out between his fingers, but most of the water stayed in his hand until he tipped it and it ran out over the body.

When the whole body was glistening with water, Harun rubbed the skin with both of his hands. First the face, then the neck and shoulders, then the chest and stomach and further down. By the time he had rubbed the feet, the water had evaporated. And the body was dry and yellow.

Like the desert.

෨◊෨

NOTE

In addition to various reference works and documentaries I am grateful to the following works: Thorkild Hansen's travel diary *En kvinde ved en flod* (A Woman by a River), Tage Skov Hansen's *De nøgne træer* (The Naked Trees), Ryszard Kapuscinski's *Shadow of the Sun* and *Salmonsens Konversations Leksikon* (Salmonsen's Encyclopedia). Much of the novel's lexical information is based on its articles.

Halvorsen's observation that damnation takes place in the great works was taken from Klaus Høeck's *In Nomine*. And Kurt Schwitter's poem, "An Anna Blume," was drawn from the book A-N-N-A, Klampen Verlag, Lüneburg, 2000. Josef quotes Frank Jæger's poem "Befrieren" (Frank Jæger, *Samlede digte*, Gyldendal, 2001).

Finally I'd like to thank my father, Jørgen Fastrup, for information and clarifications on factual details.

Karen Fastrup, June 2003

KAREN FASTRUP was born in 1967 and lives in Copenhagen. She made her authorial debut in 2000 with the novel *Brønden* (*The Well*).

TARA CHACE has been working as a translator for ten years. She has a PhD in Scandinavian literature and translates Danish, Swedish and Norweigian. She lives in Seattle, Washington.

COLOPHON

Manufactured in an edition of 1000 copies in the summer of 2008 by BookThug. Distributed in Canada by The Literary Press Group of Canada: WWW.LPG.CA. Distributed in the US by Small Press Distribution: WWW.SPDBOOKS.ORG. Shop online at WWW.BOOKTHUG.COM

BOOK
PRODUCTION
WAR ECONOMY
STANDARD

Typesetting and design by **ad.lib type+design**